3/5/09

To Dr. Rosenfeld,

In honor of our passion for understanding the human condition and our fascination with beautiful writing

With eternal and profound gratitude from your patient,

Barbara

Onion

Onion

Kate Braestrup

Viking

VIKING
Published by the Penguin Group
Viking Penguin, a division of Penguin Books USA Inc.,
40 West 23rd Street, New York, New York 10010, U.S.A.
Penguin Books Ltd, 27 Wrights Lane, London W8 5TZ, England
Penguin Books Australia Ltd, Ringwood, Victoria, Australia
Penguin Books Canada Ltd, 2801 John Street, Markham, Ontario, Canada L3R 1B4
Penguin Books (N.Z.) Ltd, 182–190 Wairau Road, Auckland 10, New Zealand

Penguin Books Ltd, Registered Offices: Harmondsworth, Middlesex, England

First published in 1990 by Viking Penguin, a division of Penguin Books USA Inc.

10 9 8 7 6 5 4 3 2 1

Grateful acknowledgment is made for permission to reprint excerpts from the following copyrighted works:
   "Triple Muse" from *Beginning with 0* by Olga Broumas, published by Yale University Press.
   "Star Dust" by Hoagy Carmichael and Mitchell Paris. Copyright © 1929 by Mills Music, Inc. Copyright renewed Mills Music, Inc. International copyright secured. All rights reserved. Used by permission.
   "Picking Raspberries" by Lisel Mueller from *The Need to Hold Still*. Copyright © 1980 by Lisel Mueller. Reprinted by permission of Louisiana State University Press.

LIBRARY OF CONGRESS CATALOGING IN PUBLICATION DATA
Braestrup, Kate.
Onion / Kate Braestrup.
p.   cm.
ISBN 0-670-82888-2
I. Title.
PS3552.R246O55   1990
813′ .54—dc20   89-40327

Printed in the United States of America
Set in Garamond Number 3
Designed by Fritz Metsch

*To my husband, James Andrew Griffith,
and to our children*

Onion

Chapter I

The baby arrived in the middle of an August night, and announced himself unequivocally as himself.

"Annnnhhh!" he said, newly emerged, and still smeared with his mother's blood, and with vernix, the white paste that had kept him from getting pruny while in utero.

I am.

Ellen, as she held her son in her arms at long last, and looked into his unfamiliar face, said: "My God, you really are."

Thirteen months later, at the end of another white-hot city summer, Ellen Elliot watched her infant son convey blond discs of sliced banana from the tray of his high chair to his round mouth. His hair was the color of butter.

The moment felt peculiarly familiar, not so much as though Ellen had lived it before, but rather as though it were a moment that she had always had an almost palpable expectation of arriving in. Ellen felt as though she had been headed for this particular moment as though, twenty-three years before, she had been shot from a cannon aimed in this, and only this, direction. "Although in fact," Ellen said, to Bert Potocka, "twenty-three years ago, give or take a month, I, Ellen Elliot, was not shot from a cannon, merely born, and not even vaginally (which might have served the metaphor) but by cesarean section."

Bert Potocka was not in the room at the time. He was in Ellen's head, a real man imagined, by Ellen, as a lover. In Ellen's mental picture of him Potocka had no face, although there was an impression of glasses, and a high white forehead.

Ellen and the baby, only Ellen and the baby (who was known to everyone as Onion) shared a small, square window's worth of dusty sunshine in the uncleaned kitchen of a rented apartment in a semi-ghetto of Washington, D.C. Onion did not require his mother's full attention at that moment, and since he knew it to be his the instant he requested it, he allowed Ellen a brief respite within the permeable privacy of her own mind. He was, in any case, intent upon an effort to master the pincer grip, as opposed to the full-fisted grab. Onion frowned with concentration, as much as anyone can frown who has not yet grown a decent pair of eyebrows.

In front of Ellen on the blue-painted kitchen table was a battered edition of the *Revised Standard Version of the Holy Bible with the Apocryphal/Deuterocanonical Books,* and, next to that, a yellow legal pad that was slightly stained in one corner with puréed apricots (Monday's lunch). Ellen picked up a pen and began to write.

"Dear Leona," she wrote. "Greetings from chocolate city, from me, from Saul, and from your god-or-goddess son, the one and only Onion. We miss you.

"I have nothing to write to you about, really. This may be a very short letter. Here is what I did this morning: I got up (alone, because Saul worked an all-nighter last night and slept over at Martin's house). I toasted two bagels for breakfast, and Onion ate one and a half, plus an orange, two cups of milk, and a baked yam left over from last night's supper. (He is, as you might imagine, a growing boy.)

"I dressed him in a diaper and a red T-shirt with MY MOMMY IS A FEMINIST imprinted thereon. We went to Kalorama Park where he played in the sandbox. I took him out of the sandbox when I saw how many cat turds were in there. We came home.

"I stared into space for a while. I drank a cup of coffee, and regretted it, as it gave me energy that I have no use for. I washed a couple of dishes, without enthusiasm, while Onion emptied the pot cupboard. I sliced a banana for Onion, and now I am here, with a second cup of coffee, writing to you."

Ellen paused to look around. Her gaze took in the stove, the refrigerator decorated lavishly with postcards, notes, lists and leaflets announcing political and cultural events which she either had not attended or would not be attending, the kitchen sink filled with dirty coffee cups, plastic baby bottles, cereal bowls and spoons. She listened to the sounds of the apartment: the drip and bubble of the coffee maker, the irritable hum of the refrigerator, the quarreling of the neighbors in the apartment next door. The walls were so thin that Ellen could smell it when one of them lit a cigarette. I am here, Ellen thought. Here I am. With Onion, and an imaginary lover. Who could be unimaginary, if that is what I want.

Ellen picked up her pen.

"You might imagine that I could write a more scintillating letter if I described yesterday's events, but in fact the result would be the same, as the events were the same, except that yesterday I didn't notice the cat turds in the sandbox, and now I think that Onion may have eaten a few. He did have sort of peculiar breath after yesterday's playground excursion. Maybe I should complain to the Board of Health.

"But I complain to you, instead. Something is happening to me, Leona, and I don't know what it is. I am sitting here in, of all places, a kitchen at ten o'clock on a Monday morning, married to a good man, mother to a fine boy, yet contemplating infidelity the way Onion contemplates his own pecker. (It makes him grin.)"

Onion began to gag over a misswallowed Cheerio, and Ellen paused again, to panic briefly before he brought it back up.

3

"*Yeagh-gah gah,*" said Onion, examining the regurgitated Cheerio.

"*Yeaggh-gag gah,*" said Ellen back to him.

"I feel . . . what? Confused. Disembodied. Disorganized. I think what I need, Leona, is a theoretical construct by which I might be able to understand what has happened to me and whether it is a good thing in general, a politically correct thing, you might say, or not. Not that sex, or infidelity, is necessarily the right means toward that end, but perhaps this depends on who I would choose for a lover?

" 'Are you happy?' you ask me.

"*Should I be?*"

"Where is your father?" said Ellen to Onion. "Where's Dada?"

Onion released his index finger from the fist he had made around a bit of fruit, and held it up in preparation for pointing at his father.

"Da da?" he said, when Saul was nowhere to be seen.

"I don't know," Ellen admitted. Onion gave her one of his gummy, wet, forgiving grins, and went back to eating.

Saul hadn't come home the night before. He had worked a double shift, and slept over at his friend Martin's apartment in preparation for another. It was not, as usual, just one thing that kept him out. Saul was a city cop, and occasionally the area in which he plied his trade would be overwhelmed with apparently unrelated, though concurrent, calamities.

"Two 'domestics,' two fender-benders, a flasher and an attempted rape," Saul had listed for her over the telephone, sometime after midnight the night before. "Then one silly bastard tried to jump off the Calvert Street Bridge, and snagged his collar on the suicide prevention fence. We got there, and found him dangling by his neck, a hundred feet or so above Rock Creek Parkway, with a couple of assholes standing around shouting, "Cut 'im loose! Let the suckuh drop!"

"Did you?" said Ellen.

"No, Marty and I pulled him up. On the way to Saint E's, Marty told the jumper that he ought to go down to the Fourteenth Street Bridge next time, where they haven't put the barriers up yet."

"He didn't," said Ellen.

"Yes, he did. The jumper thought it was funny as hell. He had a horrible laugh. How are things on the home front?"

"Onion took a poo-poo in the bathtub," said Ellen.

"Oh, Jesus."

"He was very pleased with himself. He smiled." (When Onion smiled, he did it with his whole body; everything attached to him brightened and lifted, and his eyes disappeared into creases of abandoned joy.)

"I can imagine," said Saul. "Did you wash the bathtub? With Comet, I mean?"

"Of course I washed the bathtub! I scoured it. What do you think?" said Ellen indignantly.

"Well, I never know with you," said Saul. "The other night I came to bed, and found a half-empty package of Fig Newtons under my pillow."

"I'm nursing," said Ellen. "I get hungry."

"You're a pig, Ellen," said Saul tenderly.

"Yes, well," said Ellen, unable to come up with evidence to the contrary.

"Anyway, I should be home soon," said Saul. "Kiss Onion for me."

But an hour or so later, Saul's sergeant telephoned to tell Ellen that Saul had been called to the scene of what the sergeant referred to as an "incy-dent," and that he would be spending what remained of the night at Martin's after all.

"Shall I give him a message?" said the sergeant.

"No."

"*Yag yag yag . . . ,*" said Onion.

"*Yag yag yag . . . ,*" said Ellen. How detachable fathers are.

Ellen understood fatherhood even less than she understood motherhood, and she understood that not at all.

"Motherhood," said Ellen's mother, Maude, in one of her more recent pronouncements on the subject, "is guilt from beginning to end. A guilt trip, as they say, toward what is usually a less than compensatory destination."

That was soon after Onion was born.

"And," Maude Elliot went on, "how can you call that poor child Onion? It's ghastly. It makes him sound as though he smells bad."

"He does smell bad," Ellen pointed out. "Frequently."

Onion had been christened Owen at birth, but for some reason it was a name that no one seemed to hear correctly the first time. "His name is Onion?" people would say, shaking their heads as if to clear their ears, and Ellen and Saul eventually gave up, and began to answer Yes, Onion.

"Motherhood," Maude said, "is learning to give in gracefully, even to the unwelcome."

"I wish Leona would come back," Ellen said to Onion, who was on his last bit of banana, and showing signs of wanting to get down from his high chair and practice walking. "I would like to talk to her. Or talk to anyone, really, other than you."

Onion accepted this cheerfully enough.

"It is good to speak aloud in the English of the adult tongue, and to be answered likewise," Ellen told Potocka. "Don't ever take it for granted." Ellen had what amounted to another language when communicating with the baby; not only were the words different, but the inflections were utterly so, brighter, louder, and more pronounced. By the end of a day spent talking to Onion, Ellen's palate ached.

Conversation had lately become commingled with sex as the substance of Ellen's fantasy life. Even—or especially—with respect to Bert Potocka. Actually, sex had itself unexpectedly replaced the fantasies of new motherhood some months ago. Most of those had been part memory rather than pure fantasy anyway: Sometimes, for instance, Ellen liked to imagine that she had given *birth* to Onion, that he had come into the world via the regular route, and that she had been able to pluck him up from between her legs and cradle him against her heart immediately, without anything—blankets, diapers, hours, a tender incision—between them. But those dreams slowly gave way before a chronic, uncomfortable restlessness that Ellen had not seen the likes of since her comfortable childhood self had begun to fracture into the constituent parts of an adolescent. Ellen had been aware of the change then, she was aware of it now, and distressed, but apparently powerless in the face of it.

And now Ellen dreamed perfunctorily of sex, followed or preceded eagerly by talk. She imagined words, imagined long, luxurious conversations with no interruptions save for the sipping of tea, or the consultation of reference materials. Oh, to converse! To argue, to discourse freely, to wrap lips and tongue around sentences that tingled in the mouth, and (more important) did not refer in any way to the state of someone's diapers. Besides which, in the privacy of her own mind, she had the luxury of never having to let anyone else get a word in edgewise.

Bert Potocka was, Ellen vaguely recalled, handsome in a scholarly sort of way, but she couldn't put his face on the body in her dreams. She didn't require the face, in any case, nor even the body, but just the presence. In reality Potocka spoke English, Ellen knew that, and spoke it charmingly, with his Eastern European accent. He was childless. He wore thick glasses, and was learned in physics, particularly electromagnetics.

And *was* Ellen thinking of having an affair with him, in the flesh?

She must be. She had, after all, taken the subway up to Friendship Heights, and bought new underwear at Woodies. It wasn't ordinary underwear, either, not the usual plain, white brassieres and cotton underpants printed with flowers or polka dots.

No, this time, with Saul's child heavy in her arms, Ellen picked through the racks of shiny, matching bra-and-panty sets, the diaphanous, lace-encrusted, sinfully impractical kind. Several sets of these lay, still unworn, still with all labels and pins unremoved, a guilty, silky stash in the back of Ellen's underwear drawer, behind the nursing bras, nightgowns and mismatched socks.

Potocka had been introduced to Ellen two months before in the Cantina Havana, a Cuban restaurant on Eighteenth Street, where Saul, Onion and Ellen had met for lunch one day. Saul was in uniform, and was testy, because Onion persisted in throwing black beans at him. Bert Potocka was the man who came into the Cantina Havana just after Saul had shoved himself away from the table, and stormed off to the bathroom, equipment and weaponry clanking around his hips, to wash black beans off his badge.

Professor Bert Potocka looked around the room as if for a free table, then rested his gaze upon Ellen-the-wife-and-mommy, and smiled. Ellen stared at him.

"Vat a nice baby," he said, coming close to her table.

"Yes, he is," said Ellen, feeling a peculiar, compressed sensation in her chest. "Thank you."

"And is the mother just as nice?" said Potocka. His accent made the word *mother* sound like *muzzer*. "You *look* very nice. Very beautiful, in fact, like one of Raphael's Madonnas, with the Christ Child in your arms."

"Um . . . really?" said Ellen.

"If I were a painter, I would beg you to pose for me," said Potocka. "On my knees."

"Um . . . ," said Ellen.

Saul returned, just then, and said hello to this man, introducing him to Ellen as Professor Potocka, a physics professor at Georgetown.

(Is there any person in this city that you don't know by name? Ellen asked Saul later.

One or two, said Saul.)

"I don't know how we could have missed each other," said Professor Potocka, upon hearing that Ellen had gone to Georgetown.

"Oh, she was in a different department," said Saul. "Ellen majored in theology."

"Religion," said Potocka, smiling at Ellen, "is the mother of science."

"He was a major witness in one of Martin's cases," Saul explained, after Potocka had squeezed Ellen's hand and said "Call me Bert, yes?" before he departed.

(Ellen, usually able to hold her own in at least this form of social discourse, had said "Uh," and smiled back at Potocka in a way that would have nicked Saul's heart, had he not been too busy poking a recalcitrant shred of cheese into his son's open mouth to see it.)

"What sort of a case was it?" Ellen had asked, as she watched Potocka thread his way through the maze of tables to the door.

"Child abuse," said Saul, through a mouthful of fried plantain. "He lives next door to some guy who was beating the hell out of his kids. What did he say to you, anyway, before I got back?"

"He said I looked like one of Raphael's Madonnas," said Ellen.

"Like what?" said Saul.

"A painting. You know. The ones of Mary and Jesus?"

"Oh, yeah. Well, you do, I guess. Although you have some puke on your shoulder. Do you suppose Jesus puked as much as Onion does?"

"I don't know," said Ellen.

"It's funny that he should compare you with a painting. I would have thought he would tell you you look like a quark, or something."

9

"Thanks a lot."

"Well, he is a physicist," said Saul.

"He's a well-rounded physicist. What did you say his name was?" said Ellen casually, wiping her shoulder with a napkin.

"Bert Potocka. Decent guy. Good witness."

("You are contemplating an affair with a man named *Bert Potocka?*" Ellen could hear Leona saying.)

Not an affair. Not in the usual sense. The new underwear notwithstanding. I want, Leona, to think aloud to him.

She could hear Leona: "Yeah, right."

Well, okay, Ellen conceded. He was attractive. You might not find him so, but I did. And, it would be nice to make love with a man whose hands don't know my body the way Saul knows my body, as intimately as he knows his own. Bert Potocka had never laid eyes on me before, and yet he was flirting with me, Ellen thought to herself. To put it mildly, he was flirting. I haven't had that kind of attention from a man for a long time, but I still know it when I see it.

Still, why wasn't I neuter to him, as I have been to everyone else since becoming a mother? Not to Saul, that is. Saul still wants my body for nonmaternal uses, but my body is always there, and the wanting is, inevitably perhaps, perfunctory. Saul and I make love, and we talk about the pediatrician, mismatched socks, the phone bill. Or else we skip sex, and exchange stories about our respective days instead: Mine are about feces, tantrums (mine and Onion's), the madness of the home. His are about blood, tempers, the madness of the street. When Potocka looked at me, I was taken in through the eyes of a man who had not seen blood in the past week. Who has never seen my blood. Who has never seen me bleed.

And so I fantasize. About his brain, not his body.

Fantasize. *And?* said Leona, from the back of Ellen's mind.

Onion was agitating for attention, pulling on the fabric of Ellen's skirt and smiling at her with his eight white teeth. Ellen was helpless in the face of those teeth. Ellen put the letter away in a drawer, unfinished, and took Onion into the living room to play.

"Before Onion," Ellen explained to the Potocka in her head, "I was an undergraduate student in theology. I abandoned a study of feminist hermeneutics, a senior thesis on the first and second books of Genesis, and an active role in the university's tiny cell of student feminists only when it happened that I became, with Saul, more pregnant than I ever would have believed possible."

She had begun with morning sickness almost as soon as the seed took root in her belly, and quickly discovered that "morning sickness" was a misnomer: Ellen was sick from one end of the day to the other. Endlessly sick, miserably sick, nauseated, dizzy and fat. Hers was a pregnancy of such insistent abundance that feminist hermeneutics, if not God Herself, seemed increasingly irrelevant.

"That the irrelevance was temporary, that my interest in God, feminism, Genesis and the getting of a degree had only been blunted for a time by the demands of parturition, was something I was not to discover until it was too late: Onion was born, and I was suddenly consumed with him, and had every expectation of remaining consumed forever."

"Consumed?" said Potocka.

"Consumed," said Ellen. "Eaten whole, though not unpleasantly."

"Hormones," said Maude, when informed of this.

"Snap out of it," said Leona, before she moved away. "Get a job or something. You've got to live your own life. If nothing else, do it for the kid, so he won't be a neurotic mess in twenty years, lying on a shrink's couch somewhere talking about how his mother screwed up his psyche by nailing herself to his little cross."

"Don't be disgusting. I haven't nailed myself to his cross," said Ellen.

"Ever since I've known you, girl, it's been one damned cross after another. I'm surprised there is any more room in your palms for the nails, frankly." (Leona liked nothing more than to squeeze the life out of any metaphor that came her way.)

"And are you still consumed?" Potocka asked, in fantasy. "Still eaten? Or would you like to be?" He said it lasciviously. In Ellen's fantasies, Potocka was always lascivious—respectful, of course, as befits the imaginings of a feminist, but lascivious for all that.

When Ellen went over to her mother's house for supper, or anywhere, in fact, she brought Onion. And talked about Onion. Or else, she talked about Saul, because his work was so *interesting.* She found herself explaining "probable cause" to her mother's friends, or reciting the "10-code" to a great-aunt. To her horror, Ellen found herself clipping coupons for margarine and dishwashing soap. To her horror, she found herself peeking at another woman's laundry at the Rock Creek Sudz-O-Mat, to see if her whites were whiter (they were). To her horror, Ellen had found herself telling Leona, in another letter, that she found her current life "unfulfilling."

"Oh, Jesus," Ellen wrote to Leona. "Do you believe it? That I, Ellen Elliot, former campus feminist, heretic, and suspected lover of Georgetown University's most flamboyant, frightening, black dyke, am now a housewife, and an *unfulfilled* one?"

Could it have come to this? That the other day, Ellen picked up Saul's razor off the bathroom sink, and shaved her legs? (She tried shaving an armpit, and found that she lacked the necessary coordination. Twelve bloody and unsuccessful minutes later, Ellen decided that her underarms, at least, would remain radical.)

"No, but *unfulfilled* isn't quite the right word, Leona. I can't find the right word. I try to read a lot, to cheer myself up, but it has the opposite effect. All the novels I read are about men, or childless women. There don't seem to be a lot of books that are validating my life-style, as they say. Or questioning it, for that matter. I suppose that in this post-feminist age, we're supposed to have the life-style business under control.

"What life-style? you say. Why, this motherwife routine. Of course, no one is validating your life-style either, but as a black lesbian you can claim discrimination. What can I claim? That just because my life is excruciatingly dull is no reason for the literati to ignore it?"

But my life isn't dull, Ellen thought, as she stacked blocks on top of one another into towers for Onion to knock down.

"*Oooops!*" Ellen would cry, as the blocks fell and scattered.

"*Ooo's!*" Onion would repeat, throwing his hands up in mock despair and laughing so hard he toppled over onto the rug.

I'm not bored, I'm bewildered.

Onion said *Yag yag yag!*

"Something is happening to me, Saul," Ellen said to Saul one night, after he had blundered into bed after another long shift. "I am not the same as I was before Onion, and I'm not the same as I was two months ago. I keep seeing myself from the outside, and I don't look good."

"*Hum,*" Saul replied.

"I hear my own ears," said Ellen. "I can taste my own tongue."

"Bummer," said Saul, and fell asleep a few minutes later, in the middle of telling her an incoherent story about an elderly woman who had been thrown out of a third-floor window by her eldest son. Saul drifted into the slumber of the just and welcome home, with the words "fucking asshole" on his lips.

And Ellen had rolled over, cupped her body around his, and fallen asleep also, dreaming dreams of curiously erotic vaginal births, presided over, in scholarly fashion, by none other than Bert Potocka.

Chapter II

Your body is the instrument of his birth.

Where did that disquieting sentence come from? A birth book, or a baby-care book, Ellen supposed, as what other kind had she read lately, let alone memorized bits of? (*The* Book, of course, but only very recently had she reopened that particular can of worms.)

You were given a flawed instrument in me, Onion, she told him, not long after he was born. It did not seem to be weighing heavily on his mind. He was three months old, it was 4 A.M., and Onion was half-asleep, nursing. Only the slight movement of his hand across her breast and the occasional mumbling suck of his mouth let her know that he wasn't quite ready to be put back into his bassinet.

I'm really sorry, Onion, Ellen told him.

Onion, like his mother, was delivered by a team of surgeons. Their intervention followed seventeen hours of a labor distinguished by its difficulty and by its failure to dislodge an infant who, having remained an extra two weeks inside, had already made plain his preference for Ellen's snug womb. They cut him from her, and severed the silvery cord that joined them.

This shriveled, turned black, and eventually dropped away. One day, some months into Onion's life, Ellen examined her son's navel and realized that it looked familiar. It looked more familiar, in fact, than his face had been to her at birth, a face she had expected to recognize. Onion's face belonged to him alone, but his navel resembled, of all things, the one belonging to Ellen's mother, whose unique umbilical configuration Ellen remembered remarking upon as a child.

Where was she, that she could have had occasion to notice so intimate a portion of her mother's anatomy? Ellen remembered sitting on a blue-and-white–striped sofa in her mother's house, with her mother beside her, both with their shirts hiked up to their ribs, both examining their stomachs. There was a scar on her mother's belly that Ellen knew well. It extended from below the waistband of her skirt almost to her navel, a pale pink line bordered neatly with small, white dots, the site of Ellen's entrance into the world. Ellen's belly bore no other scars, then. Ellen couldn't have been more than six at the time, so her mother must have been less than thirty, young enough, at any rate, to examine her belly button with dignity.

Ellen, at six, declared of her mother's belly button that it "looks like ice cream in a bowl, with a cherry on top." Which was the only way of describing Onion's belly button, too.

Wouldn't you have imagined that the form one's navel took had more to do with how the doctor tied off the cord than with genetic inheritance? A belly button iş, after all, just a scar, albeit from a universal and inevitable injury.

In any case, the resemblance between these two particular scars made Ellen feel sandwiched between neatly buttoned bellies, her mother's and her son's. Leona, who should have known better, asked Ellen during her pregnancy whether the umbilical cord was connected not only to the fetus's navel, but somehow to the inside of Ellen's as well? It was an unscientific idea, but a strangely appealing one nonetheless: her mother's

navel connected to Ellen's; Ellen's connected to Onion's . . .
as though the navel might retain some use as a nutrient conduit
between the unborn and the generations before, or as though
instead of individual cords, Leona imagined one long family
cord, on which mothers and children were strung through their
bellies like pearls.

Ellen and her mother, though their navels were dissimilar,
had other, matching scars upon their bellies, one each for
appendectomy, which they both underwent at seventeen, and
one each for cesarean section. Maude Elliot's cesarean scar,
however, was vertical, after the fashion of her day, requiring
that all additional children (there were none, as it turned out,
just one miscarriage and a hysterectomy) be delivered in the
same manner. The scar that Onion's excision left in Ellen was
low and horizontal, designed, Dr. Billington, the obstetrician,
told Ellen (stroking his handiwork with disconcerting familiar-
ity and pride), to be concealed beneath a bikini.

"Also," he said, "a horizontal scar will bear up somewhat
better under the strain of a subsequent pregnancy, and
possibly, *possibly*," he emphasized, "allow for a vaginal birth
the next time around.

"Don't," he added, waggling a finger at Ellen in prophylactic
disapproval, "let your feminist types convince you that you can
be sure of a nonsurgical delivery next time . . . you should be
prepared for another cesarean. In fact, if I were you, I would
count on it." He stroked Ellen's incision once more. "A
beautiful job," he said. "If I do say so myself."

But that was before things went wrong.

Her mother Maude's appendectomy was complicated by the
rupture of the affected organ. Maude spent several months in
the hospital with an open wound in her abdomen, draining pus.

Ellen's cesarean was complicated by the introduction, at
some point during the surgery, of a staphylococcus bacillus;
thus Ellen, too, spent time in the hospital, though less of it,
draining.

Maude's appendectomy scar and Ellen's cesarean scar each had a place where the neat, straight, pinkish line gave way to a puckered, pond-shaped indentation, site of the drain, and the part of both wounds that healed not by closure but rather by a granular silting, and filling in of tissue.

Afterwards, when Ellen dreamed of Onion's birth she imagined that she knew the sleek feel of the scalpel as it cut her. Ellen did actually know what a scalpel feels like as it cuts, for this was the treatment for her infected wound: debridement, the carving away of dead tissue until the pink frontier of healthy sensate flesh was reached. In dreams, Ellen confused debridement with delivery. In postpartum nightmares, they cut more than Onion from her. Their blades were too efficient, too quick, they excised more than Ellen was prepared to lose, and she would wake up sweating, aware of her closed scar, and the odd numbness that lingered in its immediate vicinity.

Ellen took the opportunity offered by one of Onion's longer, early-infancy naps to write a letter to her obstetrician.

"Dear Dr. Billington," she wrote. "Remember me?"

She wrote to tell him that, despite her satisfaction with Onion, and despite the fact that Ellen was as sure as anyone could be that the decision to perform a cesarean section was made in good faith, and was no doubt appropriate under her particular set of circumstances, Ellen still felt terrible about it.

"I wasn't sure why for a long time," she wrote, "until I realized that, all the while that I was pregnant, I had been expecting two things. One was a baby, and the other was a birth: natural, uninterfered with and transpiring via the usual route. I received the former, but instead of the latter, I had an operation."

("Ladies' difficulties," said Maude delicately, "run in our family. You should have expected it.")

Ellen remembered lying on her back, with her arms pinioned in the manner of the Crucifixion, draped in plastic tubing, begging to see her son. He was, at the time, having his chest thumped clear of fluids, somewhere at the outskirts of her abbreviated field of vision, by a contingent of green-gowned personnel.

"Then I was given morphine," Ellen wrote. "And, stoned, I was shown my son, also a placenta. Neither image remains in memory. I have a vague picture in mind of the placenta, looking like a large cow's liver, but the image is jumpy, like an old Charlie Chaplin film. I said, 'Very nice,' didn't I? Or did I sing?"

Ellen concluded this missive with assorted pleasantries and further assurances that she intended no criticism, and mailed it off.

She imagined, in retrospect, that it must have been a pretty weird letter to receive, particularly for a physician of Dr. Billington's stripe; a perfectly good technician (the infection notwithstanding) but not one for a lot of touchy-feely. To his credit, Dr. Billington did send Ellen a response, although it was a clinical one, assuring her that the cesarean had been "indicated," and that, in all likelihood, her life and Onion's life were saved by his scalpel.

Which wasn't really the question.

"What was the question?" Saul asked, when Ellen told him about this correspondence. "Honestly, Ellen, be sensible! It isn't his job to counsel you through your postpartum depression. Imagine how many babies that guy must have delivered since Onion—he probably couldn't even remember you, let alone cope with your endless emotion."

Saul, his hairy belly unscarred by his recent entrance into parenthood, did not really understand.

Motherhood was exactly endless emotion, Ellen decided. It was a state that consisted of emotion and flesh, and no intellect at all. Ellen read Dr. Spock, and *Our Bodies, Ourselves* ("Our bodies are *not* ourselves," Maude said, on seeing the latter on Ellen's bookshelf), and with that, she had done all the research there was to do on the subject. There was nothing left for her but to sit within her body and watch events transpire, sometimes as the books described them, sometimes not. In the end, no book, however assiduously studied, could possibly have prepared her for having a baby, or even for the days after Onion's arrival.

Postpartum, and her skin, suddenly released from tension and distressingly inelastic, gathered around her in waterlogged pleats. Her breasts, huge with milk, dripped lavishly, overabundant. At feeding times, milk sprayed from her nipples (leading her to the astonishing discovery that a human nipple has *more than one hole*). Her ribs ran white with it.

When she held Onion, the world beyond the hospital bed seemed suddenly inadequate, and dangerous in the extreme. Ellen would fret and weep over car accidents, famine, perverts, lead poisoning, mean baby-sitters, nuclear winter, cruel peers, the situation in Central America, kiddie porn, falls from changing tables, high chairs, jungle gyms, trees, windows, grace.

Ellen did not, in those first days at least, weep about the circumstances of Onion's birth. In a way, it was as though he hadn't been born yet, in the sense that he hadn't really separated himself from her. Onion and Ellen remained in the hospital for five days, soggily, inextricably linked by arms, hands, nipples, lips. They wallowed in breast milk, and spit-up, wee-wee, lochia, newborn poop, sweat and the tears that ran more or less continually down Ellen's face. The sadness was not unpleasant.

Ellen admired her son. He was beautiful, sturdy and sleek, fattened by his extra time inside. While the other infants in the nursery slept curled into timid shapes, Onion stretched luxuriously, snoozed with arms and legs flung out, claiming the whole space afforded by the bassinet. His back was covered with pale, gold down. His head was round, bald, perfect.

They slept. The nurses would bustle in at intervals, claiming that Ellen would drop Onion if she fell asleep with him on her chest.

"Wouldn't you like for us to take him to the nursery for you, so you can rest?" they asked.

Ellen would smile. No, no, quite all right. She would hold Onion more closely until they were gone, then she would fall asleep again. She did not drop Onion. He was everything. He was love itself. She rested.

Visitors came: her mother, bearing armloads of flowers, but curiously uninterested in holding her grandson; Ellen's grandmother, called Grummy, who refused to let go of him for hours at a time; Leona, of course, and Martin, who had just been made a detective. He cradled Onion in his massive hands, and sang lullabies to him without embarrassment.

The hospital bed was the crossroads of Ellen's life. There, Elliot relatives, Georgetown professors, activists from the Georgetown Womyn's Collective and members of the metropolitan police force took turns holding Onion, and hearing the story of his birth.

Saul arrived daily from work, handsome in his uniform. He offered dry kisses. He slept in the chair beside the bed, holding his drowsy son to his chest between his badge and his whistle, until it was time to go away again.

Chapter III

Ellen fantasized that Bert Potocka thought aloud to her about electromagnetic physics, although she remembered very little about the subject from high school, so that all of Professor Potocka's (increasingly brief and infrequent) contributions to their imaginary conversations had to do with Ohm's Law.

"If the pressure, or electromotive force, in an electric circuit is doubled without changing the resistance," he would say, with, perhaps, his hand on her knee, "the current is doubled."

"Is it?" Ellen would answer in fantasy, her breathing light, her face just slightly closer to his than it would be during a normal, friendly conversation on an esoteric subject.

"With a given resistance, the current is directly proportional to the electromotive force, my dear. On the other hand, if the resistance is doubled without changing the electromotive force, the current becomes only half as strong. With a given electromotive force, or pressure, the current is inversely proportional to the resistance. Do you understand?"

"Yes," Ellen would say.

"Ah, Ellen, Ellen, woman of my dreams," Professor Potocka would say. "I have longed for a woman to whom I could explain Ohm's Law, a woman of intelligence and wit, not to mention a fantastic ass . . . " And then they would have sex, in the fantasy, usually after a ride on a motorcycle. Ellen was not completely weird, after all.

On the other hand, it didn't take long before Ellen began to precurse, or follow, the motorcycle ride with conversational foreplay in which she was the dominant partner:

"I was most interested, just prior to my departure from academic life, in the biblical account of Genesis," she told Potocka. " 'Begin at the beginning,' my grandmother used to tell me. So I began with Genesis and, to tell you the truth (as I shall always attempt to do), I pretty much ended with Genesis as well, since I dropped out of school to have Onion before I'd really gone far beyond the beginning.

"But anyway, I began in the belief that E. S. Fiorenza's 'hermeneutics of radical suspicion' was an essential starting point for the feminist biblical-scholar-in-embryo, which is what I had the nerve to consider myself, then. I did hope, however, albeit secretly, that Fiorenza went too far in her condemnation of the Bible as a destructive document, essentially a handbook for a bellicose, racist, hopelessly misogynous patriarchy, with a false overlay of mysticism.

"Why did I hope this?"

"Why indeed?" said Potocka helpfully.

"Because, to my own surprise, my interest in theology went beyond iconoclasty. Because it seemed important. I'm sure it had something to do with meeting Saul. It is hard to be in love with a man and, at the same time, wholeheartedly condemn his sex (although men have managed to pull this one off fairly regularly over the years). On the other hand, reading the Bible in its entirety made it difficult not to. It was a discouraging experience, enough to make anyone with any sense into a confirmed radical skeptic if not an outright nihilist, and when I'd read the Bible from cover to cover, all I could do was ask myself: How on earth can I consider this the word of God? A book so clearly a document of men in the particular, and not the generic, sense and not of very nice men at that?

"So I began by saying, quite firmly to anyone who would listen, that this is not the word of God. Not even a little bit.

"But can there be, then, a word of God? And if there can, can men speak it?"

"Um," said Potocka cautiously.

"It is a rhetorical question," Ellen assured him. "As they all shall be."

"Oh, fine," said Potocka agreeably, sipping at his wine. He was always an agreeable listener.

"When I said men, incidentally, I meant *men*. I never use the word generically. And I left aside the issue of whether women can speak the word of God, partly because the answer seemed so obvious. (We're a saintly crowd, we females, in our martyrdom.) The answer to the question of whether men can speak the word was likewise obvious: No.

"But I've changed my mind. (Not that anyone cares. Except you of course, and you're imaginary. Which is pretty sad, when you think about it.) I've decided that if men cannot speak the word of God, then we are doomed."

"Doomed?" said Potocka.

"Doomed. Finito. Dead meat," said Ellen. "Male and female, we are doomed. Listen: Men have had the microphone all to themselves for thousands of years. They have been, essentially, the only human beings speaking on behalf of God, since God (in Her dubious wisdom) began speaking in us. If we can't discover anything worth saving of the male articulation of the word of God, then both men and women are doomed even if women could begin to speak the true word now. Or, even if we did a better job of it than men have up until this point."

"Why?" asked Potocka.

"Well," said Ellen, "I don't know. Yes I do. Maybe just

because it would mean that men have written (or existed) only as men, and, given the amount of time they have had to work this stuff out, it would follow that they are only capable of existing as men."

"And being only a man is a bad thing?" said Potocka, but without resentment. (He never got defensive.)

"Yes it is. Bad in human terms, bad in the sense that it will lead to human destruction, a fate which we would, understandably, consider tragic. If the fact of your sex is more determinative of the way you think, create or worship than the fact of your speciation, if we can only conclude that it is much more significant that males wrote the Bible than that human beings wrote it, we are all in deep trouble."

"Why?" said Potocka again. "I don't get it."

"Because! *Male and female (s)he created them both.* Because we are both here, and both must be here. Because maleness by itself, without the mediation of a more powerful drive toward human-ness, is inescapably pathological, and how can we survive if half of the population—and the half that has been in control—is in the grip of an intractable pathology? (Incidentally, I suppose that, although this sentence tastes strange in my mouth, unmediated female-ness is probably also pathological, although how the pathology would express itself given unlimited license to do so we don't really know. And we should probably be grateful.) We feminists, at least, are accustomed to thinking of all men as exclusively and therefore pathologically male, after all: Who wars? Who rapes? Who subjugates and violates, divides and conquers? And who wrote this dreadful book, the Bible, which is full of the aforementioned crimes committed for and by a determinedly male God?"

"Well, men," said Potocka. "Obviously. But the Bible isn't only a record of crimes committed, is it? There are some kinder moments? Miracles and so forth?"

"There are many kinder moments," said Ellen. "Which we can see as evidence of either hypocrisy or ambivalence.

Speaking personally, I would rather interpret it as an ambivalence on the part of men, a struggle, if you will, between the reality of everyday male life and behavior, and the yearning toward something finer. Still, it is very, very hard for a feminist to read the Bible whole (let alone to listen to current interpretations of it) and not conclude that extracting what a woman could find good from all that she must find bad or indifferent is more effort than the end result would be worth."

"Aha," said Potocka.

"Worse yet, this Bible was written (and interpreted, and edited, and rewritten and reinterpreted) by men *in the name of God,* with the expressed intent of elucidating that which is all-powerful, righteous and good. Men *did their best* when they wrote this book, Potocka, and if that doesn't make you think twice about your sex, nothing will. Nonetheless, if the result of all these millennia of male effort toward the holy is irredeemably unholy, without even a whisper of God, let alone a whole word, we are all *kaput.*"

"Oh dear," said Potocka. "This is serious."

"I suppose," said Ellen, embarrassed, "it is. You will be relieved to hear, however, that I have decided (not that it matters. I announce my decisions to you, Potocka, or to the dairy case at the A & P . . .) that, with a not inordinate effort, we can find a fair number of instances where men have indeed spoken the word of God . . . "

"Phew," said Potocka. "I was beginning to worry."

" . . . in spite of themselves. And that, by speaking it, they have announced their capacity to be more than male, by inference acknowledged women's capacity to be more than female, and announced thus that the world need not necessarily end in some man-made yet incomprehensible apocalypse. They haven't said all of this outright, natch. One needs to look at the way their language dreamed, between the lines, of the very hope they so ruthlessly (and rather pathetically) suppressed: that men and women are equal in an ultimate, theological sense, equal in their humanity, equal in God. I would argue, Potocka, that this hope is the very word of God that they were struggling to articulate, or was the first word, I should say, in a long and not-yet-concluded sentence of God, one which we have not—one might hope, anyway— reached the final punctuation of.

"But did they do it, or at least dream it, in this here Holy Bible? Did they try? Did they succeed? Before we throw the Bible out with the bathwater, we should make quite sure that we no longer need whatever it was that the book provided us with, male and female. Perhaps if no woman had ever derived comfort from this text, perhaps if her relationship with man and his God had been one of pure, unambivalent degradation, we might feel justified in tossing this out, and starting over. But to deny that the comfort was experienced, or that pious women have simply been duped into their piety, is to deny women their intelligence and imagination, their humanity, in a word. I decided, back when, that I would take ambivalence as hope. If men and women have felt ambivalent in their relationships, at least there is ambivalence. That is, at least the antipathy is impure."

"Fascinating!" Potocka cried. "What a woman! Ellen, please, talk more or make love to me. One or the other, or both."

Vroom, vroom.

I am really going around the bend here, Ellen said to herself, or to Onion.

"*Yag yag yag,*" Onion answered. He had his own inner life to worry about: Ellen had given him his first half-bottle of club soda, a substance which he clearly found (with careful sips, and wrinklings of his forehead) both attractive and repellent.

"*Yagh . . . ,*" he said.

Oh, Onion, Ellen thought, looking at him. Thinking of a man, one other than her husband, with her baby at her feet and a Bible in her hand. What have I done to deserve you?

·—·—·—·—·

"You're going to *marry* this man?" Leona said, her voice cracking with disbelief.

"Yes," said Ellen.

"But why, for heaven's sake?"

"Because I love him," said Ellen.

"So what? Live with him. Live with him until you stop loving him, and then move out."

"No," said Ellen. "I'm going to marry him. I'm going to stay with him forever."

"With *Saul?*" said Leona, making sure.

"Of course with Saul. What's wrong with Saul?"

"He carries his gonads outside of his body," said Leona.

"Aside from that."

"Oh, Jesus, Ellen, nothing's wrong with Saul. But *marriage!*" Leona looked so revolted as the word came out of her mouth that Ellen had to laugh. "I'm serious! How can you even think of such a thing? Don't you know what marriage has done to women, what it means for us?"

"I know what it means for me," said Ellen piously.

"He'll have the legal right to rape you," said Leona. "Haven't you read Dworkin?"

"Yes, I've read Dworkin. Isn't she that big, scary woman in overalls?"

"She happens to be brilliant," said Leona.

"Well," said Ellen, determined not to be sidetracked, "I love Saul. I want to stay with him, and have a family with him."

"I *love* Saul," mimicked Leona, in a high voice.

"You're being shitty," said Ellen.

"Yeah, well," said Leona. "You have to admit, this is a downright bizarre turn of events. All things considered. I mean, why now? Why not wait awhile? See how you feel, in a few years?"

"We want kids," said Ellen.

"Punch a hole in the ol' diaphragm, he'll never know the difference. You don't need a man for kids, you know. Not for

27

more than a few nasty moments, anyway. And even those can be circumvented with the aid of an ordinary turkey baster."

"A turkey baster?" said Ellen.

"I will never understand you heterosexual women," said Leona, warming to her argument. "How can you possibly agree to spend *one hour* with a man, let alone the rest of your life with one?"

"I love him."

"Ick," said Leona.

"Look, say congratulations and shut up," said Ellen, losing patience. "My mind is made up."

"Fine," said Leona, her voice dripping skepticism. "Congratulations."

"Will you be my Best Woman?" Ellen asked her.

Leona sighed deeply, and scratched her nose.

"I suppose," she said.

"Thank you," said Ellen, touched.

Chronologically speaking, Leona came before Saul.

"I think Leona was a prerequisite for me," said Saul once. "Isn't that a strange idea?"

Stranger than you can even imagine, my husband, thought Ellen to herself.

Ellen carried a picture of Leona in her head: of her friend, seated before the bay window in the apartment they had once shared on S Street, a window that looked out onto a ginkgo tree. In Ellen's mind, Leona would always be before that window, reading Olga Broumas's poems aloud, her teeth bright in her dark brown face, her glasses sliding to the end of her nose, with the yellow leaves of the ginkgo tree lighting up the panes behind her.

> *"Whatever is past*
> *and has come to an end*
> *cannot be brought back by sorrow . . . "*

Leona wore long skirts, and a Levi's jacket bemedaled with buttons: NUKE A GAY WHALE FOR CHRIST! WOMEN UNITE, TAKE BACK THE NIGHT. EL SALVADOR IS SPANISH FOR VIETNAM. END RACISM. LOVE A LESBIAN. STOP RAPE. WAR IS NOT HEALTHY FOR CHILDREN AND OTHER LIVING THINGS. I'M NOT GAY, MY LOVER IS. CASTRATE LARRY FLYNT. HOW DARE YOU ASSUME I AM HETEROSEXUAL? ALL WE ARE SAYING IS GIVE PEACE A CHANCE.

Leona was a hippie.

And I am a housewife, Ellen thought. We are both walking anachronisms, low tech in a high-tech age.

"And proud of it," Leona would answer. Leona was proud, marvelously so, of everything. Of her own blackness, gayness, intelligence, and radical politics. Leona was the only black person Ellen knew who wore her hair in an enormous Afro.

Ellen and Leona met, under inauspicious circumstances, when Ellen was nineteen, and Leona one year older. At the start of her junior year at Georgetown University, and on the advice of the university housing office, Ellen moved into the apartment on S Street that Leona already inhabited with another Georgetown senior named Sasha.

Leona made it clear, right off the bat, that she had no use for another white roommate. Sasha, she told Ellen, was quite enough for any self-respecting, woman-identified woman-of-color to cope with.

Ellen had to admit that Sasha could turn anyone off white people. She was very, very white, for one thing, with a sepulchral pallor and a strange dampness to her skin, like an unwholesome, chilly perspiration, and she was pudgy. She was a psychology major, a subject she pursued in order to, as she put it, "come to terms with *who I am.*"

("Who she am," Leona commented, "is creepy.")

That fall, in pursuit of self-identification, Sasha talked, sang, meditated and Rolfed her way through a smorgasbord of therapies. Which wouldn't have been bothersome, except that Sasha had a strong streak of exhibitionism in her overexamined character, and thus Ellen and Leona were forced to witness these explorations.

It wasn't too bad at first. The nude, early morning meditation on the living room carpet could be tolerated well enough, although, as Leona pointed out, it would be easier if Sasha lost some weight.

("She's a hell of a thing to find on the rug first thing in the morning," Leona said.)

The hydrotherapy was just a series of long, cold baths, irritating if one needed to use the bathroom, but otherwise okay. For a brief, blessed period, Sasha took her psyche off to campus for several hours a week, where one of the professors analyzed her personality, charged her a hundred bucks an hour, wrote an article for *Psychology Today* about her and "pluked her on the side," as Leona put it. ("Pluked?" said Ellen.)

The worst, though, was when Sasha got hooked on primal scream.

She was very enthusiastic about it, and loud. And, with the explanation that it was all just therapy, nothing to get upset about, Sasha would depart the scene of any incipient confrontation (over, say, whose dirty undies were under the bathroom sink, or whose turn it was to walk up to the 7-Eleven for milk, eggs and frozen beef-and-bean burritos), rush to her room and proceed to give vent to the most horrifying sounds.

These were not all, by any means, inarticulate.

No, little Sasha, pale, pudgy Sasha, whose most disagreeable *public* utterance was "Gag me with a spoon," howled from behind her (incompletely closed) bedroom door epithets and insults of such baroque and revolting complexity that even Leona, veteran of a childhood in Northeast Washington, was impressed.

And irritated.

"Therapy my ass," she would say, as Sasha's primal screaming echoed through the apartment, and the neighbors pounded the walls in fury. "I'm going to go in there and slap her if she doesn't stop calling me *that black, farting cunt*." Being Sasha's roommates, Ellen and Leona came in for more than their fair share of Sasha's primal wrath. (Ellen, incidentally, was usually referred to in somewhat milder terms as "That stinking, Jewish bitch," which Ellen, being Presbyterian if anything, took to be an inaccurate, but nonetheless racist, reference to her nose.)

The primal screaming, however traumatic it was at the time, did result in two fortunate consequences, neither of which had anything to do with Sasha's coming to terms with who she was. The first was that Leona and Ellen, through the shared torture of living with Sasha, became close friends. The second was that the neighbors eventually complained to the university housing office, and Sasha was removed from the apartment on S Street and sent to live in the wilds of Arlington, Virginia. She moved out just after the pre-Christmas exams, and Ellen and Leona found themselves living, quite happily, alone together.

Leona and Ellen never developed synchronous menses, which troubled Leona, as though being on the rag together was some sort of *sine qua non* of true sisterhood. Not that she had started out interested in Ellen as a sister, or even as a friend.

"You're my new roommate?" she had said, on the occasion of their first meeting, her face a portrait in politely disguised distaste.

"Yes," said Ellen, cowed.

"Well, lucky you," said Leona, without smiling. For weeks, if not months, after this, Ellen believed sincerely that Leona didn't like her, although Leona was more polite to her during subsequent conversations. For her part, Ellen didn't know what to think of Leona.

She carried a long, lethal hat pin in her Afro.

She made her own peanut butter.

She drank malt liquor on Saturday nights, down in Northeast with her multiple cousins, at a bar into which Ellen, even as a friend, could not follow her. She had seen dead people: two cousins killed, one with a baseball bat, one with a knife; and a neighbor beaten to death by her husband. She was the only child in her family, or in her family's memory, to go to college. She was good at chemistry. She was good at sports. She was good at *everything*.

Leona intimidated Ellen in so many ways that it took Ellen a fairly long time to realize that she actually liked her, and even longer to accept the idea that she, Ellen, might be worthy of being liked by someone as amazing as Leona.

Once Sasha moved out, however, and the friendship was established, it was almost as though Ellen and Leona were married. They cooked for each other, and cleaned house (infrequently) together, and went to the movies once in a while. Leona brought Ellen into the Georgetown Womyn's Collective, and Ellen discovered feminism, with a capital "F."

"It is what I have been looking for," she told Maude, over lunch one day. "A theoretical basis on which to establish a meaningful life. There are so many things that I didn't understand before, that I now understand."

"Theory is nice," said Maude, having given her mouthful of endive salad a thorough chew, and disposing of it with a ladylike swallow. "But life invariably interferes with it. You haven't lived yet. You don't know. Besides, Ellen, there is something to be said for bowing to convention. Your eyebrows, for instance."

"My eyebrows?"

"You've let the hairs between grow in, haven't you?" said Maude. "The result is mannish. Couldn't you pluck a bit, and maybe put some lipstick on? Does feminism require you to be so drab?"

"Mother . . . ," said Ellen.

"I've seen pictures of Gloria Steinem, you know. She doesn't look drab. Although frankly she could do something more becoming with her hair rather than just letting it *hang* there like that."

"Mom, how can you talk about lipstick and hair? I'm talking about justice, freedom, equality, women controlling their own bodies . . ."

"Ladies never control their own bodies," Maude interrupted flatly. "Under ordinary circumstances. It's unfortunate, but there it is. No matter what we do, our bodies are always in the way, always doing something unexpected and disgusting, just at the worst possible moment. I must tell you, Ellen, that I found it considerably easier to be a woman once my uterus was removed."

"That is a horrible thing to say," said Ellen. "Really horrible."

"Perhaps," said her mother. "But it's true, nonetheless."

"Your mother is a wild one," said Leona, when she was told about this conversation. "She has a point, though. I mean, I like my body and so on, and I love other women's bodies, but, Christ, they are a big pain in the ass. You couldn't write a book like *Our Bodies, Ourselves* for men, a whole goddam book about nothing but how to cope with your genitals. Men don't have to do anything to keep their genitals healthy, just wash 'em now and then, and remember to wear a rubber when they fuck a whore."

"Leona!" said Ellen, shocked.

"Well, it's true," said Leona. "My mother must be right. God must be a man, after all. But He's in for a big surprise when Leona Douglas gets to heaven, let me tell you. This little worm is going to *turn,* baby. You watch and see." At which point, Ellen and Leona looked at each other and said, "TURN, BABY, TURN" in unison, and laughed.

However flamboyant and outspoken she was in these personal conversations, Leona was surprisingly adept at the political games that radical life at a conservative, Catholic university required. She never got angry and was infinitely patient with the more dim-witted freshwomen who came to meetings to find out why, say, marital rape was still rape ("I mean, shouldn't a girl just kinda expect . . . that?"), as well as with the university administrators, who collectively remained in a state of chronic semi-hysteria over the possibility that the Womyn's Collective might burn bras on Healy Lawn, picket the student health center demanding birth control or (worse!) open up the abortion question on campus, a question that resembled a slightly crusted sore on Georgetown's nostalgically Catholic but otherwise cleanly and preppily secular body. Only the Right-to-Lifers picked around the edges of the issue, complacent enough in the support given their group by the university establishment, yet uncomfortably aware of how few of their fellow students (residing, as they did, in co-ed dorms, or group houses) were chaste, while none seemed to be bringing forth children. (Once, under cover of night, a particularly radical member of Right to Life planted several hundred small white crosses in Healy Lawn [the central campus green space] to represent the number of abortions which, statistically, must have been performed on Georgetown women during the year. The "graveyard" was illegal, a disconcerted administration claimed, and lousy P.R. as well, and maintenance men were quickly dispatched to remove it before any touring applicants might see it.)

Ellen was not particularly good at public relations, and she possessed none of Leona's superior organizational skills, but she discovered in herself a reasonable talent for spouting feminist cant, either verbally or in long letters to the editors of the two campus newspapers. She quickly became fairly famous as one of the two large, feminist fish in a very small collegiate (and innocent, Ellen recognized in retrospect, so innocent!) political pond.

Ellen and Leona's shared life took on a pleasant, predictable regularity. On Saturday nights, if Leona wasn't expected "downtown," they walked up to Millie and Al's on Eighteenth Street for a beer. On Sunday mornings, Leona would make pancakes, or French toast, and they would sit together in front of Ellen's ancient black-and-white television watching the televangelists, to get their ire up for the coming week. On weekdays they would walk to campus together, and sometimes across campus hand in hand, just to make the priests nervous. Wednesdays were Womyn's Collective meetings, Thursdays were Progressive Students' Alliance meetings, and on Fridays Leona, at her request, went to Black Student Alliance meetings alone.

Leona did not have a lover, then, and Ellen did not expect to find one either. The men at Georgetown, and men in general, seemed distinctly unappealing to her at the time. She avoided their eyes, and turned down any offers for dates that might come her way. Pretty soon, the word got around that Ellen Elliot and Leona Douglas were now an (unnatural) item, and after that, Ellen was left alone.

Life with Leona felt snug and good. There was room in it for thought, for her studies, and for conversation. There was time for lectures, poetry readings, books. A lot of books. Ellen was intoxicated by the books and words, by all that thought. Ellen got good grades. She felt smart. She felt clean in her body, chaste, and cool.

"I may become a nun," she told Leona.

"You have to be Catholic," said Leona. "And do Catholic stuff. And no screwing."

"Exactly," said Ellen.

She feared that Leona would find someone, "Ms. Right," as Leona would say, and that everything would change.

Everything had to change anyway, of course.

They were not lovers, after all. Just friends.

Chapter IV

When Doctor Billington, M.D., first assumed the task of overseeing Ellen's pregnancy, he took from her what he referred to as a reproductive history. "Shouldn't that be a herstory?" said Ellen, determined to be combative. She knew about obstetricians, and their wicked, sexist ways.

"I suppose it would make more sense," said Dr. Billington coolly, looking at Ellen over the rims of his bifocals, then back to the page in front of him. "Now, as I was saying . . . "

Ellen's reproductive history was extracted from her elegantly, with each event, onset of menstruation (fourteen—ick), duration of each period and the intervals between (four days and "it varies," respectively), and previous pregnancies entered neatly into its own space on a form. Previous pregnancies?

"Previous pregnancies?" Dr. Billington repeated, looking up at Ellen again.

"Uh, one," said Ellen.

Just one.

My history *is* my reproductive history, Ellen thought. Dr. Billington could chart my life and moral development by consulting that miserable form. If he wanted to. If the history he found there wasn't merely a dull repetition of other women's history.

"There isn't much variation in women's lives, you know," Maude said to Ellen, upon visiting her in the hospital after Onion was born.

Ellen had given voice to a certain eerie sense of *déjà vu;* "I was a cesarean baby, and now I am a cesarean mother. I am living your life, Mom."

"But the possibilities for lives to live are limited, aren't they?" said Maude.

"I'd like to think not," said Ellen.

"Ah yes, feminism. Well, we shall see, won't we, how your generation fares. Remember," said Maude, pointing at the ceiling of the hospital room as though comeuppance for all feminists lurked there, "something is always lost for what is gained."

"Thanks, Mom."

"You lay inside of me sideways," her mother had explained to Ellen as a child. "They called it a transverse lie. That sounds very philosophical, doesn't it? Trapped by a transverse lie?"

Impatient and uninterested in the method of her exit, or the reasons for it, Ellen, at six or so, asked, "But what happened next, once I was out?"

"Then," said her mother, "you were taken to the nursery, and I was sewn up. Later, I woke up, and saw Dr. Rabinowicz next to my bed, holding a baby in his arms."

"That was me!" Ellen would say.

"That was you. Dr. Rabinowicz said, 'Mrs. Elliot, you have a beautiful little girl.' I looked at you, saw that you were indeed beautiful, and I was so happy, I almost wept."

"You were happy to have a girl?" Ellen asked her doubtfully, since Ellen was not convinced at the time that her gender was much to celebrate.

"Of course I was happy to have a girl, I wanted a girl! I prayed for a beautiful little girl," her mother would say.

Ellen, at six, thought, Yeah, right.

"Then I made Dr. Rabinowicz count your fingers and all your toes for me, out loud, so I could be absolutely sure that they were all there."

Her mother would demonstrate, counting Ellen's fingers and toes out loud, pinching them one by one until, like Dr. Rabinowicz, she found ten of each.

"You were perfect," her mother would say.

"I still am!" Ellen would answer, holding up her hands as evidence.

Years later, having become demonstrably imperfect, on one day out of her nineteenth year of days, Ellen waited for her mother to pick her up and take her to the same hospital in which Ellen was born, in order that Ellen might exercise her right to a safe and legal abortion. It seemed a curious compression of events that she should be born, and abort, in the same place, not only in the same city but in the same building. But then, aborting one's first pregnancy is not meant to be considered an event on the same scale as being born oneself.

Ellen waited alone for her mother, seated on a couch made out of a folded futon mattress. She had only just moved into the apartment on S Street two or three days before. Boxes of books, clothing and oddments were still stacked on the floor beside her. Her roommates, Leona and Sasha, both still strangers to her, were gone for the day. Neither had been told that Ellen was pregnant, or that she would on this day become unpregnant again.

Ellen had almost told the one named Leona that morning. Leona, a tall black woman with a huge Afro and granny glasses, had been making a cup of Red Zinger tea in the tiny kitchen, and muttering chemical formulas to herself in preparation for an exam.

"Good morning!" she had said, politely, when Ellen entered the kitchen. "What are you planning to do today?"

And Ellen, with her head buried in the small refrigerator,
could only bring herself to say:

"Unpack."

Their other roommate, Sasha, Leona told her, had gone to
Chevy Chase to take part in what Sasha called a "session."

"She's a therapy addict," said Leona.

"Oh," said Ellen, not really understanding, yet.

Leona refrained from telling Ellen that her nickname for
Sasha was Fetus-Face. Which, given Ellen's circumstances, was
probably just as well.

From the front window, Ellen watched Leona walk away
down the street, her boots confident and loud on the
pavement, her arms heavy with books. Ellen was lonely.

It was autumn, a particularly beautiful time of year in
Washington. With folded hands, Ellen watched the ginkgo tree
outside the window shed yellow, fan-shaped leaves. In the
little park across the street, a man wearing several overcoats
and a plastic garbage bag slept on a bench, surrounded by
pigeons.

Ellen was anxious, even desperate, for her mother to arrive.
Ellen imagined that she would bring comfort and salvation.
The night before, weeping, sleepless, surrounded by boxes,
Ellen had said "I want my Mom" out loud. (But quietly.) Who
else's name does one call, when life outside the womb, let alone
in possession of one, threatens to overwhelm? Whomever
Ellen was crying for in the night, the mother who bore her was
not the comforting type. Maude was a good person, kind in her
own way, but not particularly helpful when it came to a crisis,
particularly one involving bodily fluids: blood, say, or tears. So
she wasn't really the ideal person to bring to an abortion, which
Ellen imagined (correctly, as it turned out) was a wet sort of
crisis, but she was the only mother Ellen had.

Ellen heard her mother, Maude, come to the door. She got
up from her seat and let her in.

Maude was wearing her black wool coat, although the air

wasn't cold enough to warrant it, and she had Ellen's grandmother, whom the younger family members referred to as "Grummy," in tow.

"Hello, darling," said Maude, and then, in a conspiratorial whisper: "How are your spirits?"

"My spirits?" said Ellen. "They're all right, I suppose."

"Hello, hello, hello," said Grummy. "Hello," she added, for good measure, then stopped speaking, and stood in the entryway, listing slightly to one side, sucking at her dentures.

"Hello, Grummy," said Ellen.

Grummy normally spent her days watching television in her own house on Capitol Hill, tied securely into a large chintz-covered chair, surrounded by cheerful Central American nurses. She had once been a tall woman, and handsome. Ellen had a photograph on her wall of Grummy, taken at eighteen, a month or so before her forty-two years of marriage to Grampa Howard would commence. All umber eyebrows, Grummy glared balefully at the photographer, clutching a bunch of flowers in her fist. In the corner of this photo, the young Grummy had written (in scratchy, black fountain-pen ink) "Blithe Spirit."

"The Howard women," Maude once remarked (a group in which Maude usually counted Ellen, but not herself), "are a sarcastic bunch."

But disease and time had pared Grummy down; she was now tiny, with a white, wispy-haired, sweetly senile head that poked forward from a substantial dowager's hump, giving her the appearance of a confused, blue-eyed tortoise.

"I had to bring her, Ellen," said her mother. "Lourdes called me this morning, her sister is in premature labor, so Lourdes had to go to the hospital and pray, that's what she said. There was nothing else I could do."

"That's all right. The more the merrier," Ellen said. She put on her sweater, and smiled at her grandmother.

"Lourdes!" said Grummy, brightening. She patted Ellen's

face. "Lourdes?" she said, as they made their way slowly down
the hall.

"No, Grummy, I'm Ellen. ELLEN."

"ELLEN," said Grummy agreeably. *"Qué tal?"*

"She's speaking Spanish," Maude informed Ellen unneces-
sarily. "Those nurses teach it to her. She remembers it better
than English, God knows why. Just ignore it."

"She's asking me how I am," Ellen said. "Luis, the building
manager, asks me the same thing every morning. *Estoy bastante
mal,* Grummy."

"Don't encourage her, Ellen," Maude said. "She's already
koo-koo, there's no sense in setting up a language barrier."

They were descending the stairs. Ellen held on to the
banister with uncharacteristic care.

"What does that mean, anyway?" said Maude. "What you said?"

"It means I'm lousy," Ellen said. "It means I feel pretty shitty
today, ol' Grummy."

"Ellen!" said her mother, shocked. "Language, dear."

"Pretty shitty," said Grummy, laughing, as Maude opened
the front door of the building, and the cool air greeted them
with a shower of ginkgo leaves.

In the car, Grummy sang the first line of "Stardust" over and
over:

> *Sometimes I wonder why I spend*
> *the lonely nights . . .*
> *Sometimes I wonder why I spend*
> *the lonely nights . . .*
> *Sometimes I wonder why I spend*
> *the lonely nights . . .*

Ellen sat in the front seat. Maude drove. She was a quirky
driver, stopping late for stop signs, accelerating with little,
hesitant taps from her right toe, and steering around corners

in a series of straight lines rather than a smooth arc. Ellen normally found her mother's driving annoying, but today, it was torture.

"Jesus Christ, Mom," she said, as her mother navigated Ward Circle as though it were a dodecahedron. "Just drive around. Just drive around."

"You're upset," said Maude. "I understand."

"Sometimes I wonder why I spend the lonely nights," warbled Grummy from the backseat.

"It's hormonal," said Maude. "I was a terrible sourpuss when I was pregnant with you."

"I am not a sourpuss," said Ellen, while, inside, she recoiled at the word *pregnant*. "Your driving is making me sick."

"It's all hormonal," said Maude. "That's the trouble with being a woman. All those hormones. My hysterectomy was the best thing that ever happened to me."

"I'm not sure that I would admit that to just anyone," said Ellen. "Frankly."

"Well, it's true," said Maude. "I think people should be honest, don't you?"

"Look out for that truck," said Ellen, although the truck wasn't really posing a threat. Maude honked her horn anyway, and the woman driving the truck flipped her a bird.

"People have become so rude, lately," said Maude. "What is becoming of us all?"

"Drrreaming of a so-o-o-ong . . . ," Grummy sang, suddenly remembering the second line.

The part of the hospital where abortions were performed was on the seventh floor, next to the part where babies were born, presumably because the same personnel were required for both.

Maude, Grummy and Ellen rode the elevator up. Ellen kept her eyes on the numbers above the door as they lit up in sequence, indicating progress. They arrived at the seventh floor, and the doors opened with a ping.

BIRTH CENTER, one sign read, pointing to the right.

FAMILY PLANNING WING, read another, pointing left. An oriental woman in a pale green uniform was scrubbing a spray-painted swastika off of the sign with a foul-smelling solvent.

"Bastante mal," Grummy observed, as Maude led the charge into the Family Planning Wing.

It was a progressive place. Kindly women, dressed in street clothes of richly colored natural fibers, batiks, folk embroidery, ethnic necklaces, greeted them in hushed voices, oozing acceptance. They seemed surprised to see Grummy, but not displeased. ("So many come in alone," one nurse-ish person whispered to Ellen. "It's great that you have this multigenerational support.")

Grummy watched, fascinated, with her wrinkled face about eight inches from Ellen's arm, as a nurse wearing large silver earrings took blood. Then they were ushered into a waiting room.

It was small, windowless, and decorated with framed posters of nature scenes: waterfalls, forests, sunsets and so forth. Grummy and Ellen sat on an orange, modern sofa. Maude sat in an armchair. Maude read *The Diary of Anaïs Nin,* Ellen read a short pamphlet on dilation and curettage, and Grummy swung her feet, which didn't reach the floor, and sang the first two lines of "Stardust" to herself. They waited for a long time.

Ellen knew that there are women who can have abortions without sorrow. At least, Ellen had heard that such women exist, and she was once having dinner in a restaurant in Georgetown, and overheard a woman announcing that she had recently had one, in the same bright tone Maude used to take when informing Ellen that she was being taken to the opera at the Kennedy Center—a tone that implicitly demanded approval, even gratitude, in the listener. Ellen heard the woman say the word *abortion,* and, even then, her clean womb cringed with an ancient, reactionary ache.

And now, about to undergo the same operation, albeit in a different spirit (if, in fact, that woman felt as blithe about her abortion as she appeared to), her womb again was aching, full of blood and the beginnings of a baby.

I could leave, Ellen was thinking to herself, reading the pamphlet closely, searching the cool prose for absolution: *There's still time.*

Ellen tried to remember the man's face, Frederick, who had contributed his milt to this unfortunate occasion. The face and its owner seemed utterly irrelevant, and even the event that had ultimately led to her presence in the waiting room seemed unrelated.

It had taken place on a soccer field.

The sex, that is. But Ellen couldn't think about sex.

Never again, she thought. I have had it with insertion, with penetration. *Insertion. Penetration.* Ellen closed her eyes, and felt her legs squeeze tightly together of their own volition.

Ellen sat in a room with her mother and her loony grandmother, waiting for an abortion, and realized that she hadn't laid eyes on a man all day. She racked her brain, remembering the car ride over to the hospital from her apartment. She remembered seeing several women in career-clothes striding along Massachusetts Avenue, a lot of stroller-pushers heading for the park, even the cop directing traffic at the intersection of Florida Avenue and Nineteenth Street, where the light was broken, had been female. Washington had turned into a city of women. Where were the men? And why did their absence seem so unremarkable, not only to her, but to everyone else as well?

There's still time, her belly said to her.

"You know what?" Maude said, looking up from her book and glancing around over the tops of her reading glasses. "I think that this is the old waiting area for the maternity wing, the place where the fathers used to wait, and smoke." She got up and paced around the room, as though taking measurements. "It looked completely different then, of course, but I think it is the same room! How funny! Your father waited, in this very room, to hear of your birth, Ellen . . . isn't that amazing?"

"Amazing," Ellen said, looking around, trying to picture her father, although he died when she was so little that she only knew him from photographs. The image she had was a queer one of a man with her own nose holding up a dead striped bass, wearing hip waders, grinning before a poster of the Grand Canyon. "Didn't they let him come into the delivery room with you?"

"Oh, no, not in those days. In those days, you labored alone. Grummy would remember, if she wasn't senile. She was here, too, you know, waiting. They waited all through the labor, and all through the operation. She and your father danced a waltz, they told me, when they heard that you had arrived at last . . ." Her mother smiled. "And then·they went out for breakfast."

But that was then, Ellen thought.

Ellen looked at Grummy, and Grummy looked at her, smiling expectantly, swinging her brown shoes six inches above the carpet. The waiting room suddenly seemed crowded with fathers in hip waders waltzing little old short-legged ladies around and around.

"Son mis zapatos más nuevos," said Grummy with satisfaction, swinging her feet.

A black woman wearing a blue denim skirt, a turquoise peasant blouse and a name tag that read "Lisa" put her head in the doorway and explained that it was time for Ellen's counseling session.

"I'm going to run through the procedure, and explain it to you," Lisa said, once they were alone and facing each other over a round, pale wood table in another, smaller room. "If you have any questions about anything at all, please feel free to ask. Don't hold back. We want you to feel comfortable."

"Fine," Ellen said.

Lisa described a standard, first-trimester abortion with the same language that the pamphlet used. Did Ellen have any questions?

Where were all the fathers?

Would it hurt? Would Ellen have to put her feet in those stirrups? Ellen hated stirrups. Ellen hated having strangers examine her vulva, as though it were her elbow, as though it weren't sacred. She hated it when the gynecologist separated her labia minora with his fingers, pinching them aside like artichoke leaves, she hated the lights and the drapes, the specula. Ellen felt sick to her stomach. She wanted badly to go home.

"Can my mom come with me?" she asked.

"Do you want her to?" said Lisa.

"No," Ellen said.

"After the procedure," said Lisa. "We will want to talk with you about birth control methods, and schedule you for a follow-up appointment, and so on."

Who set this up? This sex business, who arranged it?

"All right," Ellen said.

It was difficult not to imagine a conspiracy of men, at moments like this.

"Is that your grandmother out there in the waiting room?" said Lisa. "Boy, she's cute!"

She was cute. Ellen returned to the waiting room, which was now occupied by two additional women, one black, one white. Grummy was conversing earnestly in Spanish with the white one, who didn't seem to notice that Grummy was senile. Maybe she wasn't, in Spanish. Maude was glaring at them over the top of her book.

"*No tenemos mucho tiempo para cocinar!*" Grummy was saying, as Ellen entered the room. "*Qué tal?*" she asked, when she saw her.

"*Bastante mal,*" Ellen answered, and the Spanish-speaking woman nodded.

The black woman sat with her elbows on her knees, and her head propped on her hands. She was looking at the floor, and Ellen could see the snot and tears dripping off the end of her nose. Her own nose prickled.

There is still time, her belly told her, her frightened belly, which was making itself flat, hiding beneath her underpants. Ellen felt tight. They won't be able to get inside, she thought. Inside. Ellen was afraid.

"Ellen?" said the counselor, Lisa, reappearing in the doorway. Everyone looked up. Ellen stood, alone, and then her mother stood, too. Maude reached out and held her daughter's arm tightly.

"Will she be anesthetized?" Maude asked.

"We use a local anesthetic," Lisa said. "It won't be too painful." She had one foot in the waiting room, the other in the hall, and she rocked forward and back, forward and back, as though she were trying to winch Ellen out of the room with an invisible line.

"Why can't you knock her out all the way?" said Maude, holding Ellen back. "I think you should knock her out all the way." She spoke as though her throat were sore.

Ellen began to feel a strange sort of ache down the middle of her body. I am torn, she thought. This is the sensation of being torn between two mutually exclusive desires: My body is divided eye from eye, breast from breast, arm from arm, leg from leg. How terrible, that I can't have everything.

"It's all right, Mom," Ellen said, peeling Maude's hand from her arm. "Stay here. I'm all right."

"*Qué pasa?*" said Grummy. "*Es el programa? 'Todos mis Niños?'*"

"I'll be back in a minute, Grummy," Ellen told her.

"Lourdes?" said Grummy to her. "*Esta vez no puedo venir . . .*"

"No, Mum, it's Ellen. She'll be back soon," said Maude, regaining control.

Lisa brought Ellen down the hall to a small operating room.

She stayed with her while Ellen took off her pants and her underpants, and helped her to clamber up onto the table. She picked up Ellen's feet, one at a time, and put them into the stirrups.

Several nurses arrived, wearing green gowns over their clothes, bearing trays of instruments covered in green cloth. Unwrapped, the instruments looked like a disassembled steam engine.

"Just relax," said Lisa to Ellen. There were posters of kittens on the ceiling. A nurse yawned, covered it with the back of one hand, smiled at Ellen.

Lisa stood close to the table, close to Ellen. She smelled of sandalwood, and the same coconut hair dressing that Leona used. Suddenly Ellen remembered the smell of her new roommate, coconut and Red Zinger tea, and missed her. Tonight, I will unpack my books, Ellen thought. Missing her books. I will unpack my books, and maybe drink Red Zinger tea with Leona.

"This must be a jolly job," Ellen said to Lisa. "Watching abortions, day after day."

"I like to help people," Lisa said. "Just relax."

The doctor arrived, a man wearing a mask, and glasses that magnified his eyes, so that they seemed huge, with lashes of obscene thickness.

"You're a man," said Ellen to him.

"I'm a *doctor*," he said. "Just relax. This won't take long."

"Do you have children?" said Ellen.

"Just relax," said the doctor.

"Yes, I know," Ellen said. "They already told me." Her hands, resting beside her hips, were very cold. "You should offer us mittens," she told Lisa. "And socks."

"Of course we should," said Lisa. "Just relax now. Here we go."

·—·—·—·—·

This is what an abortion feels like: the relatively familiar splaying of the thighs, the cool vulnerability of damp membrane found by air, the fingering of lips, outer and inner, the speculum. Then there is a deep pinch, and ache, as they numb the cervix by injection, there is pain nonetheless as they dilate it with one after another of their metal rods. Then they insert the curettes, and scraping can be felt. One can hear the wet, sucking sound of the vacuum suction. The wall of the womb seems sensate, and the surface of the belly moves, quivers, vibrates. It hurts.

As they will tell you, it is over swiftly.

The doctor stood up from his stool and left. Patting Ellen's foot with one kind, gloved hand, he goggled at her through his glasses, having said: "You'll feel better sooner than you imagine."

Which was nice of him.

The nurses, over to one side, examined the extracted contents of Ellen's uterus, counting fingers, counting toes, or the first-trimester equivalent thereof, making sure that the perfect whole had been removed.

"May I see?" Ellen said, shocking them. She could not.

Lisa was gentle, close, physical, she drew her off the table with an embrace, folded her into a blanket, kept an arm around her as they shuffled to the recovery room. She smelled like sandalwood, and coconut hair cream.

Ellen sat on a cot, on a pad, bleeding, and Lisa brought her graham crackers and apple juice.

"It's all over with, now," Lisa told her.

"Did you tell my mother?" Ellen asked her.

"No, but I will," Lisa said.

(And will my mother, on hearing the news that her daughter has been delivered of this inconvenience, waltz with Grummy, and with the ghost of my fisherman father, around and around the waiting room until the Grand Canyon, the sunsets, beaches, Sequoias and waterfalls whirl?)

Lisa told Ellen to lie down on the bed. She pressed hard at Ellen's abdomen, and there was a gush of blood. Lisa went away, and Ellen was alone.

After ten minutes or so of the hour Ellen was instructed to remain in the recovery room had passed, the door opened and Grummy's face appeared around it. She put her index finger to her ancient lips and said, *"Shhh!"*

"Qué pasa?" Ellen said to her. "How did you find me?"

Grummy tiptoed over to her cot with exaggerated stealth, and clambered up to sit beside her granddaughter.

"Maude?" she said, peering into Ellen's face, stroking her cheek with a soft, dry hand. Her touch was inexpressibly comforting.

"I feel sad, Grummy," Ellen told her. "I feel horrible and sad." Ellen started to cry. "I feel really bad, *muy mal, muy, muy mal.*"

"Muy mal . . . ," Grummy repeated, stroking her cheek, patting her arm, sucking her dentures, looking at Ellen with a love that seemed to reach from behind the clouds in her mind. *"Pobre, pobre Maude. Pobre Maude."*

Ellen smelled sandalwood again, and Lisa reappeared, with her arms wrapped around the Spanish woman, whose face lit up when she saw Grummy.

"Groomi!" she said. *"Ahh, hola, Groomi!"*

"Cuidado," said Grummy, by way of greeting.

"Sí," said the Spanish woman.

"Visitors aren't allowed in this room, Señora," said Lisa. She came over to Grummy and took hold of her, gently but firmly, the way nurses do, with or without their uniforms.

"She's not really Spanish," said Ellen.

Lisa looked at her blankly.

"Never mind," Ellen said. "It's not important."

"Come along," said Lisa to Grummy with greater, though still kind, firmness.

Grummy drew herself up from her hips, and for an instant her hump was gone, and she looked like the proud old photograph of herself in another age.

"I must insist," she said, without a trace of Spanish accent. "I must insist."

Lisa took her hand away.

"I must insist," said Grummy again, pressing her advantage, and finally Lisa smiled.

"All right," she said. "But don't tell anyone."

Grummy, in evident recognition that the threat of eviction had passed, compressed accordion-style back into a confused little old lady. She ate a graham cracker, spilled a little juice on her sweater, and greeted the arrival of the weeping black patient with a radiant, insane, but apparently comforting exposure of plastic teeth.

The other women, Grummy and Ellen sat together quietly for the hour or so of recovery time. No one disturbed them. It must have been a slow day for abortions.

Grummy sang a little, but quietly.

Ellen had the pleasant thought that they had all been forgotten, that her mother and all the beautifully dressed, understanding nurses and counselors had gone home, and that the other women and Ellen might just stay there all night together, listening to Grummy's song, bleeding in peace.

But then Lisa announced that the time was up, and they dressed themselves, shook hands in an awkward, mannish moment, and then Grummy and Ellen went back to the waiting room. No one, apparently, awaited the now-unpregnant return of the other two women, who were discharged on their own recognizance.

No one seemed to be waiting for Ellen, either. Her mother had vanished.

"She said she was going out for a cigarette," the nurse in silver earrings reported. "She's been gone for about forty minutes. Want me to have her paged?"

"No," Ellen said. "That's all right. We'll find her. Good-bye. Thank you."

"You're so welcome!" said the nurse. She handed Ellen a package of post-abortion materials: sanitary napkins, instructions, a questionnaire, an appointment card for a diaphragm fitting. " 'Bye, now!"

"Good-bye," said Ellen again.

"No los cuentes!" said Grummy, waving.

"Whatever that means," said the nurse, winking.

Grummy and Ellen walked slowly out of the Family Planning Wing. Ellen thought that she might throw up, but it didn't seem like a good moment to do so.

In the elevator on the way down, Grummy looked very intently into Ellen's face and said: *"Otra vez, otra vez, Ellen."*

"What do you mean, Grummy?" Ellen said. It seemed for a moment that she did mean something.

But Grummy suddenly remembered the next line of "Stardust," and began to sing it.

> *The melo-deeee*
> *Haunts my memoreeee . . .*

They found Maude in the lobby of the ground floor, smoking a cigarette, and examining the wares in the gift shop window.

"I was trying to think of what I might get you for a present," she said.

"That's all right," Ellen said. "Thanks for coming with me."

"Of course," said her mother. "It's traditional."

Chapter V

"Genesis," Potocka mused, on another occasion. "Ah, Ellen, would you please refresh my memory? My reading of the Bible has not been at all recent, as you may know from finding me here with you, a spicy young trollop intent upon sin. Would you care for more Chablis, to wet you down for your explanation? And afterwards, would you like to tie me to this brass bed that I find, conveniently, just over there? I have a nice rope, or some handcuffs, if you prefer."

"All right," said Ellen. "But no handcuffs."

"I understand," said Potocka, lighting up a thin cheroot. (What the hell is a cheroot, anyway? Ellen wondered, and, deciding it was something akin to a cigarette, struck it from her fantasy.)

"Anyway," said Ellen, "I'm getting ahead of myself. Begin at the beginning, Grummy said, and so I will.

"The thing to remember about Genesis One and Two is that they were written around the time of David, and that they combine four or five literary strands that were certainly written at different times and places and later combined into more or less what we read today. I know that it is fashionable in certain circles to insist that Genesis is an account of the literal creation of the natural earth, but people who believe this believe all sorts of other crapola, so I won't bother going into why it can't be so . . . we can assume that, as a scientist, you know this anyway, Potocka . . . "

"Quite," said Potocka.

" . . . and why it need not be so in order for Genesis to be theologically true. Instead I would like to think that this is an account of the creation of the human earth, which isn't the same place as the natural earth. The first part of this creation was the naming of what only something human would see as chaos: *The earth was without form, and void.* The Spirit of God moved over the face of the waters and saw chaos.

"It is human—not prehuman, not primate and not animal— to perceive chaos as chaos. It is human to be disconcerted by mysteries, and to want to name, order and solve them. The ability to answer is preceded by the need to ask, comprehension is preceded by apprehension. An existential anxiety (where am I? What is this place, and what, therefore, are my circumstances?) is the only thing that could give rise to the need to order by name (this is earth, this is sea, this is sky). Only human beings need a named, ordered world in order to survive. The human God—and She was human, or at least super-human, for aren't we told that we were created in Her image?—created as She named: *And God said Let there be light and there was light.* Not particles of light, which existed anyway, just as the face of the waters existed, but the name of light, distinct from darkness. Which could also be named. (Which, in a way, makes Genesis an account of itself: it is, itself, a process of ordering and naming, describing a process of ordering and naming. Wow, voo-doo, as my friend Leona would say.)

"Interestingly, though, once a solution to the existential anxiety of our biblical ancestors is offered to them, the creation of the physical earth in all its complexity is given relatively short shrift, compared to the amount of energy lavished upon the creation of Adam and Eve. Actually, it isn't even the physical creation of these that the authors were concerned with—even questions that could have been of interest to the most rudimentary natural historian are ignored completely. Because they weren't interested in natural history, or what passed for biology, they were interested in human life, which resided, for them as for us, in human relationships. Adam and Eve's story was told in order to answer the pressing question of why human life seems so *difficult,* in ways that theologians (among others) continue to fret over to this day."

"I see," said Potocka.

"The specific aspects of human life that seemed most painful to the writers of Genesis were the series of relationships given punitive dimensions by God after the Fall. These relationships are as follows: between woman and her body (*in pain you shall bring forth children*), woman and man (*yet your desire shall be for your husband and he shall rule over you*), man and earth (*cursed is the ground because of you; in toil you shall eat of it all the days of your life . . .*) and man and death (*. . . till you return to the ground, for out of it you were taken. You are dust, and to dust you shall return*), all of which are, in effect, relationships in which a mind confronts its surroundings: including the immediate surrounding of its own body: instincts, vulnerabilities and mortality.

"We can sensibly assume that for our ancestors prior to the Fall, prior, that is, to becoming human, all of these relationships were not particularly difficult. Before the Fall we were, in essence, animals. Clever animals, perhaps, or queer-looking animals, but animals nonetheless, with the straightforward relationship between self and surroundings that animals, in their perfection, enjoy."

"Or seem to enjoy," said Potocka. "You never know."

"Well, yes. Whales, or gorillas, say, may have some existential anxieties we are too blind to recognize. But for the purposes of this conversation let's assume that an animal's relationship to her environment is straightforward, and that the loss of that straightforwardness was our unique, human curse. It should be emphasized, for example, that the rule of man over woman—patriarchy, in other words—was not part of the biblical account of God's *original* plan. There is no scriptural evidence that inequality between the sexes existed in Eden. In fact, there is evidence to the contrary: In Genesis One, having created man, *male and female he created them,* God gave both dominion *over the fish of the sea and the birds of the air and over every living thing that moves upon the earth,* and this equal partnership was a part of what God sat back, admired and pronounced good. The fact is that inequality between the sexes was specifically listed as a punishment, which argues that even our patriarchal amanuenses for God considered this inequality an aspect of damnation (and thus something that men should be none too proud of, or eager to retain).

"It is the relationship between men and women that I was and remain most interested in, of course, being a feminist, and since Genesis is an account of the inception of the relationship as well as of the relators, Eden seemed a fruitful place to begin an inquiry. There are two distinct accounts of this inception in Genesis One and Two, and which you decide to quote most has tended, over the centuries, to depend on your sexual politics. Genesis One has male and female appearing simultaneously, Genesis Two (more familiar to most of us) has Adam appearing first, with Eve later being molded from one of Adam's ribs.

"Incidentally, did you know that for years, anatomists miscounted the ribs in a male chest in order to bring what passed for science into accord with Genesis Two? And did you know further that I had occasion to discuss Genesis with at least one young undergraduate male at Georgetown University who was still laboring under the misapprehension that you could tell a male skeleton from a female one by the number of ribs it had? (And did you know, Potocka, that I *slept* with this ninny?)"

"Um . . . ," said Potocka.

"Another question you need not answer. Anyway, the feminist Phyllis Trible tells us that we should really be looking at the narrative as a whole, rather than in its separate parts, if we want to glean a satisfactory story from these chapters."

"Okay," said Potocka.

"There are a few cheery surprises in Trible's interpretation," Ellen went on. "For instance, she points out that even in Genesis Two, which has generally promulgated the least complimentary version of the arrival of woman, you can see Woman not as an afterthought, but rather as the crowning gem, the culmination of creation. God saved his most perfect creation for last, and so on."

"He certainly did," said Potocka.

"Or, you can know that the word *helper,* when God tells Adam that She has made a 'helper' for him, is not the word in Hebrew that one would use to refer to a subordinate being. The same word, in fact, is used to refer to God in another part of the passage, so Eve is offered up as at least Adam's equal.

"But the most compelling part of Trible's recombinant interpretation has to do with the time before Eve, when there is only one human creature in the world that God has created. According to Trible, we can call this the Earth Creature, or Ha'adam, and it is both male and female (or neither male nor female, since if you are both, you're neither . . . right? Does that make sense?) and it is *this,* bisexual, creature that is made in God's image. The removal of Eve from Adam's side in Genesis Two is, therefore, less an extraction of a lesser part from a whole than it is the splitting of a whole into two equal constituent parts. The sexual union of Adam and Eve, therefore, is actually a re-union, and since it is the original united Earth Creature that was created in the image of God, (hetero)sexuality is an act that, in reuniting a man and a woman, recreates that image. The metaphor is of sexual reunion as a religious event, and it is a compelling one . . . "

"Indeed," said Potocka. "As I have come to realize, since being with you . . . "

" . . . given that in sexual union, man and woman physically interlock, become, in the words of the educational book my mother once gave me on the subject, 'as close as two people can be,' and in doing so, they create somewhat as God created: They make a baby (or might, anyway) that is literally the joining (genetically) of them both into one person, a child who mingles their images in her features."

"Ah yes!" said Potocka. "Go on."

But Ellen couldn't go on. Her imagined monologue, and Potocka's encouraging murmurings, were interrupted: " . . . Oh, Onion, no, no, my darling. Don't eat the soap . . . Oh, Onion, that's all right. Mum will get it out for you . . . "

Dr. Potocka, miffed, did not wait around for Ellen to finish wiping the soap out of Onion's mouth with a soaked washcloth. He vaporized himself. Onion, with the soap taste lingering on his gums, was ready to get out of the tub anyway. The bath, he decided, was a less agreeable place than he had imagined, wherein lurked disgusting soap masquerading as something yummy, and frankly, he said (in his own way, reaching for Ellen with his dripping arms) he could do with a hug.

Ellen, embracing her fat, wet infant, abandoned an effort to reconjure an attentive Potocka. Onion's body fit neatly to hers. With his chest snuggled in between her breasts, she could feel his heart beating against her bones. His arms encircled her neck, he gave her the kisses only a baby can give, kisses so pure and sweet they could otherwise come only from God. Ellen buried her nose in her son's damp hair, inhaling the smell of her own child. I shall try to remember this smell, she thought to herself. A smell like fresh-cut pumpkin.

And me? said Potocka.

Maybe later, said Ellen.

And later, that is, the next morning, Ellen turned up in the Physics Department at Georgetown in search of the real Professor Potocka.

He was not, technically, the reason for her being in the neighborhood. Not that first day, at least. Onion's pediatrician happened to operate her practice out of the university hospital. It was a nice day, and so, after Onion's checkup, Ellen had just meandered toward the main campus and then sort of meandered into the science building. Which was easy enough to find—Ellen had taken one or two science courses there, although none more taxing than those thoughtfully provided for befuddled liberal arts types. Science had never been Ellen's strong suit, and she now approached the Physics Department with some trepidation. It was, however, comfortingly free of any odor of formaldehyde, and Dr. Potocka's office contained no fetal pigs or jars of peculiar brown things. It looked, in fact, just the way her old theology professors' offices had looked: all books, stacked papers, and coffee cups filled with stunted pencils and chewed ballpoint pens.

Potocka himself, however, was not in his office. A schedule tacked to the door explained that at this time he could generally be found in one of the larger classrooms down on the first floor, lecturing to sophomores on the fascinations of his chosen field. Ellen, with her heart in her mouth and her baby on her hip, went downstairs where she spent the next forty minutes or so lurking in the otherwise deserted hallway outside the aforementioned classroom, listening to the rich, baritone murmer of Potocka's voice accompanied by the audible scribble of frantic student pencils.

The wall between classroom and hallway was too thick to allow much of the content of Potocka's lecture to reach Ellen, but she leaned against it anyway, listening to that intoxicating monotony.

The hallway smelled like school. Chalk and ink, pored-over library books, floor wax and the elderly sponges used to swab down the blackboards at the end of the day.

"Vulnerability is the cornerstone of the temple." In the back of her mind, back where the Before Onion memories were kept, Ellen heard one of her old theology professors intoning, "You can only declare a place inviolate if it can in fact be violated, declare it sacred if it can, in fact, be desecrated. Vulnerability distinguishes the temple from the fortress. Vulnerability precedes faith." A voice, and the answering scribble of pencils, the occasional question or response.

Ellen listened to Potocka, guiltily. I love this, she thought.

She couldn't see Potocka, and he was not aware of her presence, so there was nothing especially wicked, or thrilling, about what she was doing. But a safe five minutes or so before the class ended, Ellen fled, light with unfocused affection and a foolish adrenaline surge.

The following Tuesday, Onion did not have a pediatrician's appointment, but Ellen and Onion were back in the hallway anyway.

And they were there the Tuesday after that, too, and on Thursday as well, since Ellen suddenly realized that Potocka's class, like other classes, met twice a week.

How did she justify her absence from home? She didn't need to. Saul worked the day shift all month, with overtime usually extending well into the evening. Ellen took Onion to the science building the way she used to take him to the zoo, or to the Air and Space Museum. She felt guilty for doing it, of course. Quite aside from the fact that this peculiar activity was a sort of infidelity, could hanging around in a hallway be considered beneficial for a child's development?

Onion spent the time in the hallway more or less the way he spent it at the museum: toddling about, investigating the radiators and the drinking fountains, muttering importantly to himself. Toward the end of what would be the last of these vigils, he decided to push all the buttons on the soda machine, which responded by disgorging a nickel. Onion tried to eat it. When Ellen put her finger into his mouth to retrieve it, Onion emitted a shattering scream. Ellen, panicking, stuffed the spitty nickel back into the coin box and tried to sweep Onion up into her arms to make a quick getaway before someone— Potocka himself?—emerged from the classroom to investigate what surely must have been an unusual sound in these environs. But Onion wriggled away from her, and set off down the hallway and, just as he did so, a janitor, an elderly man with whom Ellen had been acquainted during her student days, appeared at the other end of the hallway. He saw Onion. Then he saw Ellen.

"Ellen!" he hollered. "Where have you been, girl? Is this *your* little baby?"

"Um, yes . . . ," said Ellen, cantering in the janitor's direction so that he wouldn't feel it necessary to shout her name again. "Hello . . . yes, he's mine."

"Well! Would you just look at him!" said the janitor, hunkering down to toddler level and holding out his arms. "Come to ol' Henry, young feller. Come on." Onion waddled obligingly into his embrace. "He's just *fine*! Well, missy, now I know why we haven't seen so much of you lately."

"Yes," said Ellen, glancing at her watch. The class on introductory electromagnetics was due to be released. And here she was. Caught.

At what? Ellen asked herself, even as the classroom doors opened, and a gaggle of students came through them. A couple of them stared curiously at the little group in the hallway as they passed: a disheveled white woman, a laughing baby, an elderly black man in a custodian's uniform, and Ellen stared curiously back. They looked incredibly young to her. She felt old and dumpy and maternal. A stroller-pusher.

I'm twenty-three, said Ellen to herself.

"I guess you musta married the policeman," Henry was

saying as Potocka himself appeared, carrying a bunch of exam books in one hand, and looking disgruntled.

"Oh, yes," said Ellen. "I married the policeman."

"That's fine," said Henry. "Good for you. Well, I spoze I oughta go clean something. Hate to let this little tiger go, though. My littlest granddaughter's two this week. Don't I just miss her to death?"

"Um, yes?" said Ellen. Potocka was shrugging elaborately at some question put to him by the young man dogging his heels. And coming toward her. "Isn't that nice?"

"It *is* nice," said Henry. "And I'm going to Philadelphia tomorrow, for the birthday party."

"Oh, that will be fun, won't it?" said Ellen, her voice getting light and silly as Potocka approached.

"Oh, I'm looking forward to it. But anyway, here, young man, you'd better go on back to your momma." Onion allowed himself to be disentangled from the old man's embrace. Back on Ellen's hip, Onion gave her a wet smooch, and poked a forgiving finger into her ear. "Nothin' like your very own momma, is there?" and then Henry abandoned them, just as Potocka caught sight of Ellen.

"Ellen!" he said.

Ellen was so stunned that the man remembered her name that she could not reply, let alone come up with a reason for her presence there. She just stared at Potocka, addled by his grin and voice. My goodness, she thought to herself. My goodness, but he is a stone fox, as Leona would say.

"You are Ellen, aren't you?" said Potocka.

"Oh! Yes. I'm Ellen. Ellen, " said Ellen.

"I thought so," said Potocka. "The policeman's wife. And you," he said to Onion, "are Ellen's baby. What a lucky little baby boy—do you remember me? I don't think so."

"*Glaaa . . . ,*" said Onion, reaching for an exam book.

"Are you on your way to the Theology Department,

perhaps?" said Potocka. "I am headed that way. We could walk together."

"Uh, yes," said Ellen. "Yes, of course."

So they walked together. "I know someone in the theology department," Potocka told her. "Professor Schaefer, do you remember her? She remembers you."

"She does?" said Ellen.

"I asked," said Potocka, with endearing embarrassment. "About you, I mean."

He looked at Ellen. Ellen looked distractedly at the sidewalk. Onion munched contemplatively on the corner of a blue book. Two bicycles laden with books and undergraduates sped by.

"Yes?" said Ellen faintly.

"She said you were a feminist," said Potocka. "Famous, on this campus, for your radical views."

"Well," said Ellen. "It's all relative, isn't it? This is a conservative place."

"Yes. I don't know much about that. I'm afraid I'm not very political. I don't really notice much outside of my work."

"I see," said Ellen. They stopped before the red brick modern edifice of the building that housed, among other things, the Theology Department. Ellen was not particularly inclined to leave Potocka's company, but here was her excuse for being on campus, after all.

"I think I am what they call an egghead," Potocka confessed.

"That isn't such a bad thing, though," said Ellen. She took the blue book away from Onion and handed it over to Potocka. "I'm afraid my son has made a mess of this."

"That's all right, I'll blame it on my teaching assistant," said Potocka. "He drools, too."

Ellen laughed. She began to edge reluctantly toward the doors of the building. "Well, good-bye," she said. "See you around."

"Yes," said Potocka. "Oh . . . ah . . . Ellen?"

Ellen stopped. "Yes?"

"Oh, nothing. It's . . . well, you made a strong impression on me when first we met, you know."

"I did?" said Ellen.

"Of course," said Potocka. "But is that surprising?"

"It is, frankly," said Ellen.

"You are a . . . well, an interesting woman," said Potocka. "The more I learn of you, the more I think so. Your husband must tell you this often, though."

"He said you were a good witness," said Ellen, trying to remember the last time that Saul had told her that she was interesting.

"So I am," said Potocka. "But listen . . . I am thinking, might you not come back someday, to see me? Perhaps next week?"

"Um, come see you?" Ellen said.

"Come to see me. If it's convenient. You must say yes, Ellen, or I shall defenestrate myself."

"Defenestrate?" said Ellen.

"I shall hurl myself from these windows," said Potocka, gesturing extravagantly toward the red building's windows, whose windows were, as it happened, unopenable. Then, embarrassed again, he looked down at the ground, where his feet twitched. "It is what Czechs do, you know, when we are distraught," he explained.

"Oh," said Ellen. So, she thought, the man is from Czechoslovakia. A country I know nothing about. I shall have to look it up.

"Come see me here, Ellen, all right? And we will talk. Or wait, do you live near Columbia Road, where I saw you last? Is that your, er, what do you say? Neighborhood?"

"Yes," said Ellen.

"That would be better, then! You can come to my house, it isn't far. Near the zoo, Cleveland Park. Do you know Cleveland Park?"

"Yes," said Ellen, a reply too brief to infuse with lewd suggestion.

"*Glaaaaa,*" said Onion, spitting up.

"You are a beautiful young man," said Potocka to Onion, as Ellen mopped the baby's chin with a disposable wipe. "And you are so much more coherent than my students . . . oh, I don't like my students today." He tore a scrap of paper out of the back of an exam book and scribbled a telephone number on it. "Call me up, and we will arrange, yes? We will have lunch. Your husband, will he mind?"

"Well, I wouldn't *tell* him," said Ellen without thinking, taking the paper and stuffing it into Onion's diaper bag. She looked up just in time to catch the tail end of Potocka's smile.

But why? Ellen thought, driving home, later, having wandered in and out of the Theology Department (managing not to see anyone she knew there). With Onion in his car seat behind her, singing, Ellen wondered: Why does he want to see me? I'm a mother, for heaven's sake, not one of those jazzy young things in his class. Why would he smile like that at the idea of being alone with me, why would he offer to defenestrate himself in my name, for Christ's sake? That may be what Czechs do, but surely not with such paltry provocation? And how does he even know who I am?

"Saul," Ellen asked him that night, when he got home from work, "what did you think of me, the first time you saw me?"

"What did I think of you?" said Saul. "I thought you were a hot ticket. I thought to myself: Here she is, a woman of substance, the woman I want to marry. Could you shove the butter over here?"

"That's nice," said Ellen, shoving butter. "But would you have remembered me? I mean, did you want to see me again, just from seeing me that one time?"

"You know I did," said Saul. "I called you, didn't I?"

"That's right, you did," said Ellen.

"Damn right. I asked you out on a date, and I copped a feel.

65

What more do you want? Will you pass me the meat loaf? Listen, the last time you washed my underwear, they came out green. Did you wash something green with the white stuff? I wish you'd be careful, Ellen. I don't turn your underwear green when I do the laundry."

"You don't do the laundry," Ellen pointed out.

"Sure I do!" said Saul. "I mean, okay, I haven't for a while, I guess, because I've been doing a lot of overtime, but I *used* to do it a lot. I taught you to do laundry, remember? Careful separation is the key to proper laundering, as my mother used to say."

"All we ever talk about is laundry," said Ellen, bursting into tears. "Laundry, and diaper rash, and whose turn it is to wash the dishes. Mine," she added. "Always mine. To hell with it."

"What do you want to talk about?" said Saul.

"Nothing. Electromagnetics."

"Electromagnetics?" said Saul, bewildered.

"Feminism. *Feminism!* Hah! Ha ha ha ha!"

"We could talk about feminism," said Saul.

"Yeah. Eat your meat loaf. I'm going to bed."

"That sounds nice," said Saul, waggling his eyebrows at her, trying to be friends again.

"I don't want sex," said Ellen. "Just so you know. I don't want sex."

"Fine," Saul sighed. "Boy, Ellen, you are really a barrel of laughs lately, you know that?"

Ellen did know it. But there wasn't much she could do about it.

She asked herself: What am I doing here, married? And is it enough to remain married out of pure ennui?

No one she knew was married. (Her mother had been, of course, but Ellen had no memory of her mother as a married woman, and her mother seemed, by the time Ellen got around to thinking about it, too much herself to ever have promised to join hand and heart with someone else.) Part of it was that

many of Ellen's friends were gay, and part of it was also that
Ellen was relatively young when she married Saul, and those
of her peers who still retained some interest in men were as yet
too wholly concerned with postgraduate plans to be thinking
much about settling down to domesticity with one.

And it is domesticity, isn't it? Ellen said to herself.
Sometimes it feels alien and recognizable at the same moment,
as when Onion and I are sitting together out back in the alley,
watching Saul wash the car. I sit on the stoop in my skirt, with
Onion crawling around on me, and I watch Saul lather the car
and hose it down, whistling, with the muscles showing under
his white T-shirt, the cuffs of his khaki pants rolled up. (He
makes jokes now and then about how the only thing holding
the car together is Turtle Wax.)

I feel at those moments as though someone ought to be
shouting "BUY WAR BONDS" or playing Cole Porter on a
gramophone. As though domesticity, or marriage itself, is an
anachronism that I have somehow fallen into. It bothers me a
little that sometimes those moments seem peculiarly beautiful.

Reality intrudes, of course. Saul, between the washing and
the waxing, pops a tape into his ghetto blaster and Grace Jones
bites out "Art Groupie." And I, Ellen Elliot, having come of
age in these odd years, say: I am *married,* as though the word
is too slippery to speak with the same mouth that can lip-synch
"Pull Up to the Bumper, Baby." I used to dance to Grace
Jones, Ellen thought. With Leona I would dance, in black. It
is hard to imagine June Cleaver shaking her booty to that
stuff, but I used to. Still can, in odd moments, if only to enter-
tain my son.

I am married. To a man. We are a nuclear family in a nuclear
age; the two may just be incompatible.

·—·—·—·—·

Ellen was, frankly, unprepared for living with a man. She had
never done so, for one thing, not since she was a little girl,
before her father died. Men, she discovered (if Saul was

representative, as he seemed to be), have quirks. They are strange.

"He reads on the toilet," she wrote in a letter to Leona. "First, he announces that he is going to the bathroom, and announces what he is going to do there, loudly, so I won't be laboring under any misconceptions: 'I'M GOING TO TAKE A DUMPSTER!' he says. (I am told, by reliable sources, that Martin does this, too, so I believe that offering an announcement when one is about to perform a biological function may be a peculiarity of men in general. They announce their farts, too, also their orgasms. They have to make sure you're paying attention.) Then he sits on the can for half an hour or so, reading.

"Now, I ask you. Does it take half an hour to perform a complete catharsis of one's digestive system? When you do it, Leona, does it take that long? Certainly not. Five minutes, max, not long enough to read the table of contents, let alone a whole issue of *Modern Policework* cover to cover.

"My theory is," Ellen wrote, "that since men do most of their bathroom stuff standing up, it's a real treat for them to sit down, so they like to make the most of it."

"That's stupid," said Saul, when she told him this. "I just like to relax in there. It's comfortable, and peaceful."

Onion howled bitterly if left outside the bathroom when Ellen was inside, and usually was able to persuade her to open the door. Once in, he liked to sit on her lap, yank the towels down off their racks, pull all of the toilet paper off the roll, or, if discouraged in this, he liked to wipe industriously at Ellen's knees with a little piece of toilet paper, in imitation of her more private cleansing.

"That's the kind of thing we won't tell him when he's an adolescent," Saul said. "That he tried to help his mother wipe herself."

Onion was not interested in helping his father wipe himself, nor did he pester Saul to be taken along wherever Saul went. "It's just a stage," Saul told Ellen. "He's at his Mommy-stage, and he wants to be with you all the time. He'll grow out of it."

When will I grow out of *my* Mommy-stage? Ellen asked herself.

At night, Ellen was loath to leave Onion in his crib. She was still having vivid dreams, during which, as Saul would say, "you yakked yourself blue in the face about Onion."

One night, Ellen dreamed that she was tossing Onion high into the air, and he was cackling with delight; she awoke to discover that she had, in fact, been tossing Saul's arm up and down, and he was not at all delighted at being entertained in this manner. Quite the opposite. Then, another night, Ellen dreamed a terrible dream in which Onion was sleeping beside her in bed, as he had when he was newborn, but that he kept rolling inexorably toward the edge, and the floor was a very long way down. A howling Ellen clung to him with both hands, as hard as she could, but Onion kept twisting away from her, and toward that awful abyss. She woke up when Saul's shouts of pain penetrated her unconsciousness: Ellen had been holding Saul's head with two frenzied hands, clawing at his ears, gripping his nose and eyesockets, as he attempted sleepily to extricate himself from her grasp.

"Maybe we need separate beds, like Lucy and Ricky Ricardo," said Saul after this painful episode.

One for you, Ellen thought. And one for Ellen and the baby.

Come see me, said Potocka. And we will talk.

"Anyway," said Ellen to Bert Potocka, in fantasy, "you understand what I have been saying about Genesis, don't you?"

"Of course," said Potocka. "I am an intellectual, after all. And your opinions fascinate me."

"Do they?" said Ellen.

"Naturally."

"Hum," said Ellen. "Well, anyway. "

"But I am becoming impassioned. I have waited so long for you. Oh, Ellen," said Potocka, leaping astride his motorcycle and kick-starting the engine. "Do not force me to defenestrate myself, Ellen, in the name of my unholy desire for you. *Pull up to my bumper, baby.*"

Or something like that.

Chapter VI

Ellen's mother said to Ellen, the first time she saw the apartment on S Street, "Do you know what I like best about it?"

And Ellen said what.

"I like that blue table just there, with the vase of gladiolus on it, against that green, green wall. Such a strong, bright flower, particularly juxtaposed against the planes of blue and green." With her hands, Maude defined blue and green planes in flimsy karate chops.

Ellen said, "Well, I like the sink in the kitchen best. It drains well."

Although, in fact, Ellen had not been unmoved by the vase of gladiolus on the blue table against the green, green wall. She had, after all, been the one who had painted the wall, pushed the table against it, and positioned the vase thereon. Furthermore, the thing Ellen actually liked best about the apartment was the big, multi-paned old window, with the ginkgo tree just outside, shivering its fan-shaped leaves against the watery glass.

"Good plumbing is very important," she said to her mother.

"Oh, Ellen, you're so marvelously practical," said Maude. "So unlike me. So like your father."

(Maude professed to have only grim memories of Ellen's father, who had died thirteen years before, so Ellen did not take this comparison as a compliment.)

"You're very male, you know," Maude went on. "Or perhaps masculine. Yang, rather than yin. Appolonian, as opposed to Dionysian. Do you know what I mean?"

"Unfortunately," said Ellen, "I do."

Maude was definitely not masculine, was certainly yin rather than yang, and was Dionysian to a fault. She knew it, too. And was pleased with herself about it.

Ellen, on the other hand, did take after her father, at least in appearance. And there she was, living with a lesbian, albeit in platonic circumstances, so her mother's announcement that Ellen was more masculine than feminine made Ellen very nervous.

Leona's sexual preference also made Ellen nervous, although she tried to suppress this feeling with what she hoped was an inconspicuous lack of success. Being a lesbian, she knew, had already caused Leona a lot of grief. And Ellen wanted to be supportive of her friend.

Leona "came out" to her family in a fairly spectacular manner: she shaved her head.

What she had in mind at the time, as she would later tell Ellen, was a photograph taken just after the liberation of Paris from the Germans, of a French woman whose head had been shaved courtesy of a vengeful populace as a sign that she had consorted with the enemy.

("What enemy did you consort with?" said Ellen.

"I necked with my cousin Bobo," said Leona. "My first, and only, heterosexual encounter."

"Did you like it?" Ellen couldn't resist asking. "With a boy, I mean?"

Leona shrugged. "It was okay," she said. "But not worth repeating.")

Her hair, which had previously been styled in something

approximating "white" hair, was chopped away with a pair of kitchen shears, and the remaining fuzz was shaved down to clean scalp. Leona was sixteen years old.

Leona's mother, whose name was Florette Douglas, and who was a decent, church-going woman, but not easily shocked, said, "Lord, child, what did you do that for?"

"Men," said Leona succinctly.

Mrs. Douglas, who was sitting, as was her custom on Sunday afternoons, in a Star-Glider rocker on the back porch of her house down on Fourth Street, said: "Is this some new fashion? Are the other girls doing this, too? For men?"

Leona stamped her foot and said, "I'm not doing it *for* men, Mom, I'm doing it against them. I don't like men anymore."

"Well, who does?" said Mrs. Douglas, and laughed. "But you have to put up with them. It's God's plan, and it's for sure that *He's* a man."

"God is not a man," said Leona, losing her temper, bursting into tears. "God is not a man."

"He is," said Mrs. Douglas. "And if you'd come to church now and then, instead of hanging around playing basketball all the time, you'd know that. None of the other girls play basketball all the time. Just you."

"Well, at least I'm not PREGNANT," said Leona.

"This is true," said Mrs. Douglas philosophically. "I guess I should count my blessings."

Men, however, far from being put off, were perversely attracted to Leona's hairless head. Not the ones in her neighborhood, who had heard the rumor that she was undergoing chemotherapy for a mysterious disease, and thus steered clear of her, fearing contagion, but the men up around Dupont Circle where all the bookstores, weirdos, faggots were, where Leona found herself increasingly drawn; these men, to Leona's acute annoyance, thought her baldness was sexy.

Complete strangers stroked it without asking, "for luck," as one old white dude explained to her. A fetid little man with a nasty giggle thumped it with a salami outside of the Astro Deli, after which incident Leona had taken to wearing a hat.

("No matter what you do, there will always be some asshole who thinks you did it just for him," Leona would later tell Ellen.)

And: "It's like some fantastic, great, hard breast," the first woman Leona slept with had breathed, kissing Leona's parietal lobe with considerable reverence, and wetness.

That was a one-night stand.

As they say.

After which Leona decided that she might be a pervert, but she wasn't a freak, and she let her hair grow back. She did not, however, go back to straightening it, or rolling it, or otherwise abusing it. She let it grow long, and fuzzy, and soft, fed it a little Fro-Glo Coconut Hair Cream now and then, and otherwise ignored it.

Ellen thought it was beautiful.

Ellen thought that Leona was beautiful, and wondered whether that meant that she, too, was a lesbian?

This was all pre-Saul, back in the shades-of-gray days, as Ellen would later come to think of them. It was a time in Ellen's life when lesbianism was definitely beginning to seem a simpler, gentler, and safer sort of sexuality than the heterosexual one that Ellen had recently begun to explore, with disastrous consequences.

Ellen, in the dark days, pre-Saul, and pre-Leona as well, had had more of Maude in her than she liked to admit. She wasn't particularly pretty, of course, and she had none of Maude's instant, electrifying charm. Maude, as Ellen liked to say to Leona, and later to Saul, really knew how to be a woman. But Ellen knew how to flirt. Well enough, anyway.

Well enough for what? Why, for men to want to sleep with her, of course. Ellen had been a very naive young woman in many ways, when she launched herself forth from her mother's old house on Macomb Street, and went to live in a dormitory at Georgetown. She imagined, having had no life experience to the contrary, that a willingness on the part of a man to engage her female body in intercourse signified, if not affection, at least overwhelming desire for her, for *Ellen*. It took her a surprisingly long time to discover that many young men do not require themselves to feel either affection or overwhelming desire in order to sleep with someone, and they don't really even need to know who that someone is. The somebody can even be a *something*. For example, one man of Ellen's acquaintance informed her, without embarrassment, that he had once had sex with a watermelon.

Wrap your mind around that one, Ellen later said to Leona, who tried.

Here is the technique, for the uninitiated. The melon in question is left out in some sunny spot (in this case, the fire escape in the back of a co-ed dorm which had in better days housed nuns), until its interior temperature approximates that of a resting, or perhaps slightly aroused, human body. Next, an orifice is incised into the melon, one of a size corresponding to the dimensions of the would-be user. And then, Ellen was informed, you violate the watermelon at will.

Fortunately for Ellen's peace of mind, the man who told her about this was not a lover of hers, although he had made suggestions in that direction which, had he not been foolish enough to confide in her about his fruit fetish, Ellen might have taken him up on. She did agree to other suggestions from other men, however, and was displeased, generally, with the outcome.

But Ellen did love the game. She loved the game of letting herself be convinced, the game of sidelong glances, casual accidents of contact, fingers and shoulders, hips and hips, and the innocuous remarks spliced oddly by the different, uneven breaths she took while playing. *I'm majoring in theology,* she would say, her voice exhaling sex, inhaling sex. *I'm writing a paper on the Song of Songs . . . would you like to read it?* Breathing, with her voice light. Imagine, she would think to herself, in retrospect, being able to infuse a conversation about the Trinity, say, with lewd suggestion.

Still, toward the end of this phase in her life, Ellen played her part in the game more as a reflex than as a response to any internal stimulus—interest, say, or desire. It got to the point where Ellen no longer knew what she desired, she knew only her part and the satisfactions (fleeting) of knowing when she had played it well.

"Imagine all the energy I put into it," Ellen said later to Leona. "When I might just as well have walked up to any one of them and said 'Wanna screw?' and gotten the same results. What a waste of time."

"Men suck," Leona would reply. But Leona loved to hear about the bad boys in Ellen's life. "This is all so alien to me," she would say. "I can't relate, but it is fascinating. 'How White Straight Folk Get It On.' It's a sociological gold-mine. I should write a paper on you."

"You wouldn't get an A. This is a white, straight world, after all. To everyone but you, this is old news," Ellen pointed out.

"Well, okay. But tell me again about the guy with the spitty lips, the one who thought he looked like Richard Gere, and kept posing in front of venetian blinds like he was in the movie poster for *American Gigolo*."

Or else she would want to hear about the complete stranger who approached Ellen at the end of a long wedding reception and handed her a card with his phone number on it. "I'm worth getting to know," he had said to Ellen. "And I'm sure you are, too. Give me a ring sometime."

"I'm worth getting to know!" Leona would crow. "Where do they get this stuff?"

Ellen knew she left quite a lot out of her narratives: all the stupid things she had said, for instance, and the times when she had been mean to some perfectly adequate young man just because it was a game, and not real.

I wasn't such a great lover either, Ellen had to admit, from the calm space of her relationship (?) with Leona. I did not behave well, or even rationally. Hence the excess acquiescence, hence the lack of birth control. Hence the abortion. Later on, once Ellen had become pregnant with Onion, with the pregnancy that she could allow herself to keep and rejoice in, Ellen looked back in horror at the carelessness with which she treated her body. If men used her, she had to admit she had also used herself, albeit for different motives. Motives inexplicable, even to herself, and perhaps more perverse in the long run than the simpler male motive of wanting sex with anyone who caught the eye.

Intercourse itself was a very peculiar way to conclude the game, Ellen thought, even at the best of times. All the words and breaths, hints and promises, the sidling of eyes, all in service to this brief, undignified, damp immemorable exercise that seemed to be wholly outside the context of the moments that preceded or followed it. Without context, it seemed idiotic, and shameful. Ellen often wished, quite sincerely, that she had never slept with anyone but Saul. Ellen thought of those times in her life as being so disgusting that it was hard for her to think about the men she had slept with, or to number them.

And should I count Leona? Ellen wondered.

Oh, God.

She never told Leona about the abortion. Ellen did not discuss the matter blithely in restaurants, nor did she bring it up at Georgetown Womyn's Collective meetings as yet another result of the depravity and general worthlessness of the wombless sex.

The man in question, the one who had impregnated her on the cold turf of the university's soccer field, was a medical student, and seemed to think a lot of himself, and Ellen, being young, took this to be a sign that she should think a a lot of him, too. She fell halfway in love, or far enough to justify sleeping with him. This was a mistake, and not only when seen through the prism of its sequelae.

The medical student, whose full name was Frederick Ortega Plimpton, concealed his middle name from Ellen, and from everyone else at Georgetown, because he didn't want anyone to know that his mother was Mexican. He preferred to be thought of as undiluted WASP, and went to great lengths to convince Ellen, at least, that he was possessed of a distinguished lineage, unmarred (as he apparently saw it) by non-Anglo blood. Ellen did not find out until afterwards, and it was then that she remembered the first night in his room, during which, in order to make conversation, Ellen had asked Frederick about a photograph of a pleasant-looking, dark-haired woman that was pinned to his bulletin board.

"Who's that?" she asked idly.

"The maid," said Frederick O. Plimpton. *The maid!*

Ellen cringed at the memory of it.

What a sweet baby it would have been, though: three quarters miscellaneous European, one quarter dark-eyed Mexican. Ellen, who loved babies, especially those with dark eyes, missed that pregnancy badly sometimes.

Leona heard about Frederick O. Plimpton, minus aftermath. She heard about him as the man who made love to Ellen any time, any place, but always with his eyes closed. He was the one who would disappear into himself during their interludes together to such an extent that he wouldn't notice it when, say, Ellen's head was being knocked against the headboard of his bed.

"I tried to tell him," said Ellen. "I would tap him on the shoulder, and say 'Excuse me, Fred? You're killing me, Fred.' He never heard."

"Maybe he thought you were coming, in a genteel sort of

way. 'Oh Freddy, I'm seeing stars,' " said Leona, chortling. "Concussion mistaken for ecstasy. That's heterosexuality for you. Did you try shouting 'LIGHTEN UP, ASSHOLE!' right in his ear?"

"No," Ellen admitted. "It would have been impolite." At which Leona would sigh, heavily, and declare that she despaired of Ellen, no shit.

"What did you see in this guy, anyway?" Leona asked.

And Ellen had a sudden memory of being kissed by Frederick O. Plimpton, kissed firmly, with her body pressed between his body and the wall of an otherwise deserted classroom in the medical school building. Under the fluorescent classroom lights, beneath a detailed anatomical poster of the inner ear, Frederick Plimpton looked at Ellen with impassioned eyes, and, taking her chin in both his heated hands, he pronounced her *hot,* urgently *hot.* The memory of that urgency even now was enough to make Ellen less than sincere when she rolled her eyes and said, for Leona's benefit, "I must have been crazy."

She must have been, although it is hard to resist someone who finds you "hot." Or it was for Ellen, who was not beautiful, and considered herself yang rather than yin, Appolonian as opposed to Dionysian, and not much good at being a woman, really.

("Whatever that means," said Leona, when Ellen confessed to this inadequacy. "Christ, you just *are* a woman. It isn't a part that you play, you know. If you've got boobs and a pussy, you're a woman. Right?"

"Right," said Ellen. "Right.")

Ellen had held her breath when she told her mother that her roommate preferred women to men in matters sexual and otherwise. She need not have.

"Oh, splendid," said Maude. "Just what I would have recommended."

"You would?" said Ellen weakly, having spent all of her air

on the word *lesbian*, which had lent it an additional two or three syllables.

"It's so much more *aesthetic*. And, Ellen, are you this way as well?"

"No, Mom," said Ellen.

"I would have done it myself, in my youth," Maude said, as though discussing depilation. "Converted, that is. Except that I enjoyed penetration."

"You did?" said Ellen, flabbergasted.

"Yes of course. The other thing, though, that I can't understand is: How do you know when it's over?"

"When what's over?" said Ellen.

"Well, the encounter, dear! I mean, if you have two ladies, who can experience climax any number of times . . . how do you know when to stop? The good thing about having sex with a man is that you always know when it's over."

"I suppose," said Ellen.

"But it was this problem of penetration that held me back, really," her mother explained, tidying up the line of her lipstick with one dainty pinky. "Back when any of this was an issue, I mean."

"Well," said Ellen, entering, she believed, into the spirit of the conversation. "It is possible to be penetrated by something other than a penis."

"Ellen, *please*!" said Maude, appalled. Ellen had stepped over Maude's particular invisible line into what Maude considered to be impropriety. Perhaps the *p* word had done it.

Anyway, later on, once the requisite half hour or so had passed, and Ellen's *faux pas* had been laid to rest, Maude said, "If one had any degree of rational choice in the matter, *anyone* would choose to live with a woman, wouldn't one? Women are so much more polite. But nature throws passion in the way. I envy you, my dear, because you are a passionless person."

"I am not passionless," said Ellen. "How can you say that?"

"Well, you live with a woman, don't you?" said Maude. "It's very sensible, I think."

"Yes, but I'm not a lesbian," said Ellen. (Cursing herself, because it came out "leh-heh-hehsbian" again.)

"You could be," said Maude. "One can hope."

Imagine a mother who says that to her own daughter! Most mothers, normal mothers, try to discourage homosexuality in their offspring. At least Leona had something to fight against in her family; some honest homophobia instead of Maude's peculiar brand of acceptance.

"Do you think it's true?" said Leona, when Ellen told her of this conversation.

"You mean, do I think she's right, and that I am gay?" said Ellen.

"Yeah," said Leona, who was making an omelet at the stove, and had her back to Ellen.

"I don't know," said Ellen to Leona's back. "Do you want me to be?"

"I don't know," said Leona.

Chapter VII

"What did I do to deserve this?" said Maude. "That is what I asked myself, during my labor with you."

"Yes," said Ellen. Pregnant with Onion, and reaching back, as tradition dictated, to the generations before her for information on this supremely (not sublimely, according to the aforementioned generations) female event. "But what is it like?"

"It is like vomiting," said Maude.

"Oh, Jesus, Mom!"

"Well, it is. That same, dreadful loss of control. It's very unpleasant."

"Just unpleasant?" said Ellen. "Not, you know, transcendent or mystical in any way?"

"Not as I recall," said Maude. "And I've never actually known of any women, friends of mine, you know, or Grummy, who have described it as anything but awful."

"Oh," said Ellen. "But that was then."

"And this is now," said Maude. "Yes, yes, I know. Feminism has changed everything. If it has changed this, though, I'll eat my hat. Grummy, by the way, once told me that she was convinced that she was going to die when she had Aunt Sarah.

When I came along, she was a little less frightened. Of course, more women did die in those days. When things went wrong, there wasn't any way out."

"Well, but things don't go wrong that often," said Ellen. "Nature doesn't make that many mistakes, does she?"

"Nature," said Maude, "is not a she. Nature is an it. Remember that, and you'll spare yourself a lot of grief."

"Oh, Mother," said Ellen, vowing to herself not to return to this particular font of feminine wisdom anytime soon.

·—·—·—·—·

The second week that Ellen spent in the hospital after Onion was born, the stay required by the infection in her cesarean incision, was the pits.

The first week, Ellen and Onion had stayed in a room with yellow-painted walls, and a sunny window with a view. Nurses hovered, ready to help at the first sign of fatigue, thirst, difficulty with lactation, or crumpled bed linens. Pretty little candy-stripers would appear in Ellen's room at frequent intervals offering juice, compliments for the baby, or a quick plumping of the pillows. Dr. Billington, with his little flock of residents tagging behind him, would turn up, examine her incision, tell her that everything was fine in such a way that Ellen herself could feel responsible for this fineness, and briskly pat the mattress beside her foot before departing. In retrospect, Ellen couldn't figure out why she had been in such an all-fired hurry to leave.

Ellen and Onion came home, the first time, to an apartment of astonishing cleanliness: Saul had worn himself to a frazzle giving his nesting instinct (the one instinct Ellen showed no signs of whatsoever) full rein. Onion's bassinet (a wicker laundry basket) awaited him, luxuriantly padded with clean blankets, and assorted cloths printed with lambs and bunnies.

Onion was put to bed. Ellen was put to bed, while Saul busied himself making her nutritious dinners: homemade bread and chicken soup. When Onion woke up, Saul brought him to Ellen and sat with her while she nursed, kissing her now and then, and kissing the baby. It was wonderful. It would have been even more wonderful except that Onion had, in the space of time provided by the car ride from hospital to apartment, learned to scream, relentlessly, and for no apparent reason. Ellen, used to a sleepier, cuddlier Onion, was frantic with the sound, and was made more so when Onion refused to take comfort of any kind, not her arms, not her voice, nor even her breast. The only thing that seemed to help was when Saul would strap Onion to his chest and take him out for long walks around the neighborhood, giving Ellen quiet, but also making her sad.

"I want to go, too!" she would wail, when Saul and Onion returned from these excursions. "I want to go with you!" But she was horribly weak.

They spent two days in this way at home, followed by a third day on which Ellen awoke to discover that the lower front portion of her nightgown was mysteriously wet with . . . something. At first she thought it was errant breast milk, or lochia gone astray, but examination of the sources of these two relatively benign fluids showed that there was not sufficient leakage of them to account for her soggy state. Ellen did, however, notice in passing that her cesarean scar looked peculiar, and when she looked more closely, she saw (to her horror) that it no longer even looked like a scar. It was, to be precise, *coming open.*

"Saul," she said. "Saul, look at this."

Saul looked. "That does not look right," he announced.

He called the doctor. "Billington says we're to go to the emergency room right away, and he'll meet us there."

"Right now?" said Ellen. "Did he say what he thought was happening to me?"

"No, just that we should go now. Right now."

Ellen changed out of her soggy gown and put a clean diaper over what was apparently about to become an open wound.

They gathered up Onion and his accoutrements, and drove back to the hospital.

Dr. Billington had not arrived at the emergency room yet. They waited awhile. Ellen reclined on an examining table, and Saul hitched half his ass onto the corner of it, and perched there, holding Onion. Saul told Ellen amusing anecdotes about his work, reported on the comings and goings outside their curtained cubicle, and held Onion up to Ellen's breast so that he could have his lunch. Finally, Dr. Billington arrived. He took one look at Ellen's stomach and said, "The incision is infected. We're going to have to open it back up."

Which they did.

"Oh, honey," said Saul.

"I'm so sorry," said the E.R. nurse to Ellen.

And Ellen cried, because it hurt when they slit the half-healed wound apart, and because a smelly, pinkish water ran out of it, down over the side of her belly, and in the creases between her legs.

Thus, Ellen's postpartum crying jag was destined to continue for another couple of weeks at least, although the tears were no longer a delicious response to maternal affection, bathos, memory or love. Now, readmitted to a dreary, blue-walled hospital room without a view in some forgotten corner of the Ob-gyn ward, Ellen plain blubbered.

Onion spent the additional week in the hospital as well, although he was not considered a patient, and therefore no nurses hovered nearby, ready to whisk him away to the nursery every time he cried. The nurses had apparently given up on hovering altogether, in fact, or else were saving their hovering time for the more attractive patients at the other end of the ward, the maternity ward, a place Ellen longed for with desperate nostalgia. Every two hours, a team of wretchedly clean, healthy, cheerful residents and medical students would arrive to stand over her body, chatter about the Redskins and debride the wound. People delivered inedible meals. A whistling man wheeling a cart would arrive in the early morning and drop off a plastic-wrapped bundle of clean sheets, which Ellen usually wound up putting on her bed herself, since if she didn't, no one would arrive to do it until two or three in the afternoon. By which time, of course, two or three debridement sessions would have smeared the bed with blood and pus, and littered it with surgical gloves, and the wrappers from innumerable gauze bandages.

Onion, who remained beside her in a hospital bassinet, was a comfort; he reminded her of what the point of all this was. But he cried quite a bit, confused, no doubt, by his peculiar surroundings, and by his mother's gloom and impotence. There was no way to leave him to "cry it out," the solution Maude recommended, even had Ellen's overactive conscience allowed her to do such a thing. So she carried him around and around her small room in the darkest hours of the night, hunched over in deference to recent surgery, awash in self-pity. She changed his diapers. She bathed him in the tiny sink in her hospital bathroom. She nursed him. And all the while, she longed for sleep, for a clean white room in which to heal, for help, for deliverance.

Dr. Billington turned up once in her room, and found her in her usual flood of tears.

"Why are you crying?" he said, standing, as was his habit, as far away from her bed as he could get without actually being out in the hallway.

"This is not the way I pictured it," said Ellen, sniffling. "Having a baby, I mean."

"Well," said Dr. Billington. "You have a healthy child, and that's the main thing."

"I suppose," said Ellen, trying her best to be comforted. Dr. Billington hovered for a few more minutes, and then, as if on a sudden inspiration, he picked up a box of Kleenex off a bedside table, and handed it to Ellen.

"There," he said.

"Thank you," said Ellen. "Thank you very much," dutifully blowing her nose. Dr. Billington smiled, pleased to have been of help.

Saul came every evening, of course, and stayed as long as they would let him. He brought treats: new underpants, a new nightgown (white, sprinkled with yellow flowers), a couple of bottles of Budweiser, Sushi-to-Go from the Yosaku Restaurant. He held Onion, bathed and changed him, took him for walks out in the hallways of the hospital. He was tired, too, back at work (having used up his leave on Onion's birth and homecoming), and drained from manifold stresses. His eyes had purple hollows around them. He looked like a raccoon.

"I wish they'd let me sleep here," he would say to Ellen, pointing at the other bed in her room. "I don't sleep well without you."

Ellen didn't sleep well without him, either. She hated the hospital, hated the doctors, she hated being infected. Her wounded body revolted her.

"I'm not brave at all," she told Saul. "I used up all of my courage on labor. I don't have any more. I just want them to knock me out, and wake me up when it's all over, and my body is whole again."

On the last day of this hospitalization, Dr. Billington showed Ellen and Saul how to "dress" Ellen's wound. It required no more scalpel debridement, but was still open, healing from within. It had to be packed, four to six times daily, with damp gauze. Dr. Billington demonstrated this procedure, taking the end of a piece of gauze and prodding it deep into the hole in Ellen's flesh. The end of his gloved finger disappeared up to the second knuckle.

"I don't know," said Ellen, feeling the back of her throat contract into a gag.

"We can handle this," Saul said to her, although his face was slightly green. He took the next piece of gauze and pressed it in. "No big deal."

"Oh, Saul," said Ellen. She was discharged the next day into a typically Washingtonian August afternoon. The air was a hot, swimming soup of bacteria hungry for open wounds and the unhealed navels of newborn infants. Onion howled his outrage at being forced to live his first days in such a climate all the way home.

For the next three weeks, Saul packed, unpacked and repacked Ellen's wound, coming in from work whenever possible in order to do so. Ellen smiled, sometimes, at the memory of Saul in uniform, putting on his latex gloves, talking about "maintaining the sterile field," and offering encouraging reports of "granulation," and healing. The packing, which hurt quite a lot when Dr. Billington did it, was magically painless when Saul was in charge.

And Ellen did begin to feel more capable of coping with Onion, and more relaxed about his fits of crying, while Onion seemed to slowly get the hang of extrauterine existence, and thus he cried less.

In retrospect, however, Ellen saw that it really took at least six months before she felt herself again, more or less. And even now, she felt that the experience of giving birth to Onion and associated traumas had sapped her, removed some vital elasticity from her makeup leaving her weak, and consumed with cowardice. Ellen's body was strange to her, she was not comfortable in it.

"It made you feel vulnerable, that's all," said Saul, when Ellen told him about this. "It happens to guys on the force, after they've been wounded, even if the injury wasn't all that bad. Being hurt reminds you that you can be hurt even worse than you are."

"How long does it take them to get over it?" said Ellen.

"Sometimes they don't," said Saul. "Sometimes they have to quit, because they can't handle the job anymore."

I can't quit, Ellen thought to herself. Motherhood, as my mother would say, is a job from which there is no resignation.

Which is what she wrote to Leona in the first letter she sent out to Oregon, not long after Leona departed.

Two months or so after Onion was born, Leona announced that she was moving. She was, she said, tired of Washington, and tired, furthermore, of the self she was required to be in Washington.

"Everyone here knows me too well," she told Ellen. "I want to go where no one knows who I am. Where I don't have to be what I was at Georgetown, or what I am here, the token black dyke in a white chick's circle. Or downtown either, where I'm some kind of educated freak. I want to go someplace where I can reinvent myself."

"Hum," said Ellen, not sure at all of how she, Ellen, would go about reinventing herself. I would probably reinvent my pelvis, she thought. I'd make it capable of a normal delivery.

Leona decided on the West Coast because her brother lived in Los Angeles, and also because there was a large gay population out there, and it was therefore "cooler" than, say, South Dakota. Oregon was selected because the poet Olga Broumas lives there.

All of which apparently made sense to Leona, although Ellen, already becoming conservative in her motherness, thought Leona was out of her mind.

"But also," said Leona, having explained all of the above to Ellen, "to be perfectly frank, I think I need to get away from you for a while."

"From me?" said Ellen.

"From your life," said Leona.

"What's wrong with my life?" said Ellen.

"Nothing," said Leona. "That's just it."

Within a few weeks, Leona was gone. Ellen received a letter not long after her departure. It was mostly a description, in glowing terms not characteristically Leona's, of the new, all-female commune that Leona had joined out in Oregon.

"I have finally found a place, here at Sisterspace, where I am really happy," Leona wrote. "All the sisters here are cool, very intellectual, very accepting. There are a number of lesbian couples, one pair who have been together for over two years and are basically married, some others who have been together almost that long. These are such harmonious, empowering relationships, and I am envious."

Yeah, yeah, thought Ellen.

"I am sleeping with a womyn named Saffron, she does most of the cooking for the group.

"I was talking to everyone at our last Sistermeeting about you, telling them about how you have to get up with Onion a couple of times a night. We all agreed that it would be really interesting to see how one's mind works under that kind of stress, and to see what kind of creative flow can come from interrupting normal sleep patterns. Saffron and I have decided to wake ourselves up on purpose, and write down our thoughts, on somewhat the pattern of a baby's feeding schedule. Maybe you could write your thoughts down, too, and we could compare."

I already know what my thoughts are, at 3 A.M., nursing Onion, Ellen said to herself. It's only one thought, actually: SLEEP. I WANT SLEEP.

Imagine. Imagine *choosing* to wake oneself on "the pattern of a baby's schedule." Imagine choice.

"The other night we had a poetry reading," Leona's letter went on. "We read Broumas, of course, and Adrienne Rich, and some of a sister named Alicia's work—some very sapphic stuff, a lot of erotic images, etc. We got into a fascinating conversation about the relationship between poetry and lesbian sexuality, and whether they both shared a common wellspring and source. So many poets, womyn poets, are gay."

Sure, Ellen thought. They're the ones with time to write. How many poems is ol' Saffron-the-group-cook cranking out, I'd like to know?

"Thank you for the photos of Onion. He sure is blond, isn't

he? We don't have any children here at Sisterspace. Not yet, anyway, although we've had some roundtable conversation about the best ways to go about overcoming the obvious difficulties in this regard . . . "

Ellen put down the letter, unfinished.

It is not Leona's fault, Ellen said firmly to herself, that she has found another way than mine. It could have been my way, too. I had the option, once. I could have chosen freedom, when it was offered. It is not her fault that Leona does not (yet) understand how it is when choice is circumscribed for one, by passion.

Which only goes to show how foolish Ellen had become, in the aftermath of Onion's arrival, that she would not see that Leona, of all people, would understand precisely this; that all choices are circumscribed by passion, the passions of a lesbian woman no less than those of a heterosexual mommy, who also chose, and did not choose, her place.

Chapter VIII

"And what of this sexual union," Potocka asked of Ellen. They had finished the embarrassing part of the fantasy. Potocka had been untied from his moorings on the brass bed. The motorcycle was quiet in the corner, out of gas. Potocka, deprived of his cheroot, was making due with Grand Marnier, sipped the way a cat takes milk from a saucer from Ellen's left sacral dimple. "Does it not leave out homosexuals? Are they incapable of imaging God in their pairings?"

"Sexual union," Ellen began, "in its reality is not a means toward imaging God, or, I should say, isn't uniquely or inevitably a means toward that end. It is simply a fairly rich and satisfying metaphor for all our various fumbling attempts to re-create God's image, attempts which tend to consist of otherwise ordinary activities committed toward extraordinary ends. These attempts are, I think, as a principle, characterized by a striving for union and creation, but not only the biological versions. Keep in mind all of the miserable heterosexual pairings there are, the bad marriages, the incest, the abuses, the rapes. One can hardly characterize intercourse per se as something that images the Creator! In fact, heterosexuals may go through entire lifetimes without trying to achieve a Holy

Union in their acts, and rapists are trying for just the opposite—for disunion, for an affirmation of Otherness. Which is not good. Which is evil. If anything, in fact, sex is far *less* likely to be performed in an attempt toward the image of God than almost any other activity I can think of. Which makes sense, somehow, doesn't it? Perhaps because it is so supremely desecrable.

"Anyway, the world is created of unions, syntheses of chemicals, of molecules, or one substance plus another, or plus forty substances, unions encased in unions, unions disuniting and forming up again. Human beings, in what can either be called reverence or hubris, have an impulse toward creating unions, imaging our God by imitation: let us join this color with that on a canvas, this word with that on a page, or this people with that people, let us form something greater than the sum of the parts and indefinable by them: a painting, a novel, or nation. This is what God did, after all: took just one more collection of cells and gave it conscious life, made it considerably more, and, through the consciousness of people, imparted "more" to everything a human being can perceive. (It is we, that is, who think light is more than the sum of its particles, not the light itself that thinks so.) Doing so makes us happy. Paint on canvas, words on paper, people grouped roughly in the same geographic area and following the same rules, but more than these. How much more is the anxious question that keeps us from contentment.

"We are, ourselves, more than the matter and energy we are made of—aren't we? There is our doubt of God, and our impulse toward self-creation.

"We also have an impulse, I am afraid, toward disunity, and maybe necessarily so. It is from dissolution, as Bakunin reminds us in another context, that the constituents for creation are made available. In Genesis, for instance, the Ha'adam *must* be split apart in order for God to be imaged as the result of a conscious human act—sex, in that context, but not only sex. We must have a sense of ourselves as separate from others in order to paint, to write, or to love. We have to be separate in order to yearn for reunion, be it with an individual, an audience, or a cause. You could argue that God and Evil are just opposite ends of the continuum produced by consciousness: Consciousness, by allowing you to know simply that you are separate from others, plops you down in the center of the continuum and you can move toward bridging distance, or toward increasing it. God is our vision that complete reunion is possible, Evil (or just 'badness,' if we wish to avoid melodrama) is the rejection of that vision. And perhaps it comes from a jealousy of self: if I unite with you, I shall lose who I am." (A bell should have rung in Ellen's mind at this point, but she was distracted by Potocka's tongue, and she lost her train of thought for a moment.)

"Go on," said Potocka. "Uniting, remember?" He picked up the bottle of Grand Marnier and poured himself another shot.

"Um . . . yes. Right. Okay . . . It is a very human evil after all. It is why Eve ate fruit from the tree of knowledge of good and evil, she had to know good and evil, who she was and who she wasn't. She was too smart not to want to know, but what she found out was painful.

"Paul, the so-called thirteenth apostle, writes: *'There is neither Jew nor Gentile, neither Greek nor slave, neither man nor woman for all are one in Christ Jesus.'*

"But *only* in Christ Jesus, I would amend, or *only* in God. Only God is one, only in God are unions perfect. The Ha'adam's descendants can never be two-in-one, or more-in-one, undivided, nor can anything we make. Perfection shall always be something to be striven for, as strenuously as if it could be achieved, although it can't. Because we can't uneat the fruit, or unknow that we are not one with God or with each other. The best we can do is to image God, imperfectly, in whatever human unions we create."

"Let us create a human union," said Potocka. "Let us strive." Pressing Ellen over onto her back, let the liquor run where it may.

"You're missing the point," said Ellen. "Well, okay," she said.

· — · — · — · — ·

"Love is, from beginning to end, an embarrassment," Maude said.

"Heterosexual love, maybe," Ellen had answered, smirking.

"I thought you were a heterosexual," said Maude, smirking back.

"Well, I am," said Ellen, in some confusion. "But not by choice."

Later on, Ellen came across the phrase "a lesbian in spirit," and seized upon it eagerly. But: "Cop out," said Leona, when Ellen repeated the phrase to her. "I've heard straight chicks describe themselves that way. All it signifies is that they are willing to shun men so long as they don't have to give up any of the perks that go along with having one around. The ol' tube steak, you know, or the money."

"Tube steak?" said Ellen.

"Either you is a dyke, or you ain't, baby," said Leona, rubbing her hand across Ellen's shoulder blades in affectionate amusement. "Either you is or you ain't."

Ellen believed that the spring she spent living with Leona was the most beautiful she had ever seen. The whole neighborhood seemed to be caught up in a frenzy of gardening. Daffodils, jonquils, forsythia bloomed first, and everywhere you looked it was as though a child had gone berserk with a yellow crayon, coloring every unpaved patch of ground. Then the tulips came up, like lollipops, and other flowers as well, ones that Ellen couldn't name, but which stopped her cold on the sidewalk with admiration when she saw them blooming ferociously in someone's yard.

In the damp spring evenings, Ellen and Leona began to take

long, nocturnal rambles around a city that seemed to have grown suddenly benevolent toward its female citizens: no catcalls broke the fragrant air, and no one mugged or molested them, or even spoke to them.

On these walks, Leona would recite poetry:

> *Once the thicket opens*
> *and lets you enter*
> *and the first berry dissolves on your tongue,*
> *you will remember nothing*
> *of your old life.*

"My first year at G.U.," Leona told Ellen one evening, "I hadn't 'come out' on campus yet, and I didn't know anyone, let alone any other gays, and I was feeling very, very vulnerable."

"Me, too," said Ellen. "Although I wasn't gay, of course."

"Of course," said Leona. They were sitting close together, on a picnic table just outside the circle of light formed by a streetlamp in Kalorama Park. They were watching a couple of people walk their dogs. Ellen could feel Leona's heat, and take in Leona's smell with every breath: the sweet coconut Fro-Glo, and the slightly salty scent of Leona herself.

"I felt very black," Leona continued. "There weren't all that many black people on campus, then, and none of the women appeared to be feminists, or even *Democrats,* for crying out loud. And everyone seemed to think that I was really weird."

"You are really weird, Leona," said Ellen, draping an arm across Leona's shoulders.

"Well, I know. But I was lonely, nonetheless."

"I wish I had known you then," said Ellen.

"Yeah. That would've been nice," said Leona, patting Ellen's knee. "Anyway, as I was saying, I was feeling very uncomfortable. The one place I really felt good was in this drawing class that I took. No one stared at me there, because even a weird

black chick was less interesting than what we were supposed
to draw."

"What did you draw?"

"Nudes," said Leona. "We drew nudes. Mostly women."
And she waggled her eyebrows at Ellen, and Ellen laughed.
"Anyway," said Leona again. "There is one kind of drawing that
is apparently de rigueur in beginner's drawing classes, one
where you just stare and stare at the figure, and let your hand
describe everything you see, without looking down at the
paper."

"Isn't it hard to make it come out right?" asked Ellen. "The
picture, I mean?"

"Well, you aren't really trying for a picture that someone
else can look at," said Leona. "The idea is just to look carefully,
see totally each inch and ripple, and try to translate what is
before your eyes into the stroke of the pencil on paper. It was
quite a lot like making love to a woman."

"It . . . um, it was?" said Ellen. Her arm suddenly felt heavy
where it lay across Leona's back, but she couldn't bring herself
to suddenly remove it.

"Yeah," said Leona. "In that there is no emphasis on a
finished product, and no artificial distinctions between the
parts that you . . . draw. You are drawing the whole body but
incrementally, with as much interest shown a rib as a breast, an
ankle as a round ass. You just draw hands and feet, nipples and
eyebrows, make your pencil move around knees and throat.
You don't stop." Leona smiled, looking down at her hands.
Her eyes slid up sideways to catch Ellen's eyes then dropped
back again, shy.

Ellen thought to herself: Leona is the most beautiful woman
I have ever laid eyes on.

"What do you mean, you don't stop?"

Leona turned and looked at Ellen full in the face. She
smelled wonderful. Her white teeth shone in her dark face.

"You don't stop," she said, her voice low enough so that Ellen had to lean in closer to hear her. "You go on."

Ellen shivered. She could feel, with a mixture of pleasure and horror, a slow, delicious roiling in her belly, the circling tickle of desire. It crept from below her belly button up toward her ribs, spiraling out toward her breasts.

Ellen drew back and leaped up.

"I'm hungry. Let's go get some ice cream," she said, trotting off toward Columbia Road.

With an exclamation, a kind of a laugh, Leona followed her.

After the ice cream, they walked down to a bar on P Street, and settled into a booth for a drink. Ellen chattered madly about something or other, some minor logistical problem she had been having in locating a room in which to hold the next Womyn's Collective Discussion Group. Something like that. And Leona just sat, listening to her, tracing the carved initials in the wooden tabletop with a slow finger and smiling.

At some point, though, with a courage born of alcohol, Ellen felt the old Maude Elliot genes begin to clamor within her: *This person is attracted to you,* the instinct said. *Flirt! flirt!* and she could hear the difference in her breathing, and the strange inflections this gave to her speech, and could feel her own eyes sliding, up to catch Leona's sideways and back down again, and up. *I'm thinking of asking the Student Activities Office if we can reserve that room over in the Reiss building for the rest of the year* . . . she said, inhaling sex, exhaling sex. *What do you think?* A question infused with lewd suggestion.

Jesus Christ, she said to her own, fuzzy mind. I don't even know if this is correct, if lesbians respond to this kind of crap. Maybe this is all totally wrong, and Leona thinks I'm out of my mind? Which I am. I must be.

Just then, a man approached their table. Ellen remembered him later as being small, and rather oily, an uglier, inebriated version of Frederick O. Plimpton. At any rate, this man asked Ellen to dance, and Ellen refused.

"What are you, fa . . . fa . . . faggots?" said the man.

"Yes," said Leona.

The man shook his head, pretending to pick an obstruction out of his earhole with one short pinky. "Did I hear you say that you two are . . . are . . . "

"Gay," said Leona. "Lesbians. Now fuck off."

The man staggered back a full step, as though punched.

"But that's not right," he said. "It's not natural. It's yang and yang! IT'S YANG AND YANG!"

"Yin and yin," said Leona, a stickler for detail.

"Faggots!" shouted the man. "Faggots, faggots everywhere! It's getting so that a real man can't get some woe-man when he needs it bad . . . " and so on.

It was, as Leona later pointed out to Ellen, an inauspicious place for such a diatribe, given that the majority of the other bar patrons were, if not outright faggots, at least wobbling in that direction. Which Ellen hadn't thought of. She had been frozen, throughout the incident, with panic and claustrophobia.

The man left the bar once it was clear that he wasn't going to make Ellen and Leona see the error of their ways. Whatever mood had been brewing before his arrival on the scene was destroyed, in any case, and Ellen and Leona paid for the drinks and made their way back to the apartment in a thoughtful, mutually respected silence.

Ellen found herself avoiding Leona for the next several days, finding it suddenly necessary to go visit her mother, or to have coffee and cake ("*café y la tarta . . .*") with her grandmother on Capitol Hill. Leona, too, was spending an unusual amount of time elsewhere; in the library at Georgetown, or down in Northeast with her family. They were, however, slated for a joint appearance at Leona's parents' house for lunch the following Sunday, and thus they could not simply keep avoiding one another.

On the way downtown in the car on Sunday, Leona said, "I think we should talk about it, sometime."

"Talk about what?" said Ellen, but then she said, "Okay. Yes."

"Not right now, though," said Leona.

"Right," said Ellen.

Florette Douglas had put on a good meal. There was roast beef and mashed potatoes and string beans, and gravy all over everything. Ellen, coming from a family of non-cooks, was in heaven.

"I like a good eater," said Mrs. Douglas, watching Ellen with approval. "And she's so thin . . . Leona, does that little girl eat enough?"

"I eat constantly, but not like this," said Ellen.

John Douglas, Leona's father, sat next to Ellen. He was a quiet man, and said almost nothing throughout the meal other than requesting salt, or butter, or ketchup. Ellen was glad to be beside him; he was an undemanding dinner companion, and she felt as though that was just what she needed. Leona kept shooting meaningful glances at her across the laden table, while Mrs. Douglas chatted about the other Douglas children—two brothers and a sister, all older than Leona, and about the church service she and her husband had attended that morning. Both topics seemed to be loaded ones.

"It was all about accepting the gifts Jesus gives you," said Mrs. Douglas. "About not fighting the will of Jesus, not struggling against what is yours from Him . . . Stop and smell the roses, the minister said, when you find that you are standing in the Garden. There is strength in the Garden for the work of Jesus, if only we'd recognize it once we were there. Didn't you think it was a fine sermon, John, honey?"

"Uh-huh," said Mr. Douglas.

"It's just like I was telling your sister the other day, Leona, I said, 'Cecelia, you've got to just give in to what God gives you, and save your fighting for what in this troubled world goes back against God's will . . . ' That's what I said to her. Cecelia," Mrs. Douglas explained to Ellen, "is having a little family trouble."

"She can't stand her kids," said Leona.

"Now, Leona, that isn't quite right."

"She can't stand them because they are a big pain in the ass," said Leona. "You've said so yourself."

"Well, they are a little wild," said Mrs. Douglas. "They need a little discipline, but that isn't the same as saying she can't stand them."

"She can't," said Leona.

"What they need is a father. I never will forgive that man for walking out on Cecelia and those little children. Finding the right man, girls, is half the battle, and you have to believe he's out there. If you find the right man, everything else falls into place."

"There's no such thing as the right man," said Leona. "Other than Dad, of course." Mr. Douglas smiled at his daughter, and Leona smiled back.

"Well, anyway," said Mrs. Douglas. "Alfred and Nancy are going to have a baby any minute. Did you know that, Ellen? Alfred sells insurance out in Vienna, Virginia, he's doing fine. His wife is the sweetest girl you ever met, and is just so pregnant she can hardly see straight. Those last weeks, my lord, they are the hardest, you just feel so big. I remember carrying Leona, and how she used to butt her little head right up into my heart. She was breech you know, came out feet first. Anyway, Alfred and Nancy, they're hoping for a girl, aren't they John? But they don't really care either way, as long as it's healthy. And what if it's not? Alfred says a baby isn't like a car that you return if it doesn't work right. You take what Jesus gives you, that's what Alfred says. Finding Jesus was the best thing Alfred could've done, don't you think so, John? I wish John Junior would find Jesus, or find himself some nice girl and settle down. Last we heard, he was out in California, trying to break into acting, but there aren't that many jobs for black people, and that dirty-mouthed Eddie Murphy gets most of the ones there are. I wonder what his mother thinks of him. More potatoes?" she said brightly to Ellen, who accepted them gratefully. "So," she said then to Leona. "What are you doing with yourself these days?"

"I'm in love," said Leona, looking hard at Ellen.

"That's nice, dear. Do I know him?"

"Mother, I'm gay," said Leona. "Remember?"

"Still?" said her mother, while Mr. Douglas chewed diligently at a mouthful of roast beef.

"Of course, still!"

"It's so hard to keep track."

"I'm in love with a woman," said Leona, slowly and distinctly.

"What does she look like," said Mrs. Douglas.

"She's tall," said Leona, looking at Ellen. "Quite tall."

"That's good," said her mother. "You can wear heels."

Which Florette Douglas found very amusing, and Ellen actually did, too, but she tried not to laugh, because Leona looked so angry.

"You don't know anything about it, Mother," said Leona. "It isn't a laughing matter."

"Well, maybe not. I don't know," said Mrs. Douglas. "I just wish . . . you make everything so hard on yourself, Leona, maybe because you're so smart. My smartest child is sitting right over there, across my own dining room table, and sometimes," she said, looking at Leona and shaking her head, with Leona's own tender smile, "I just don't even know where Leona came from. You always think your children are going to be like you are, but they aren't at all, they're only like themselves, especially Leona. Jesus sent me some kind of daughter, I think."

"We all have our crosses to bear," said Leona sourly. Just then, John Douglas swallowed his food, and spoke.

"I think," he said, "that everyone has to find his own way to heaven. That's what I think." He looked around the table, as though he hadn't realized that he had spoken aloud. Embarrassed, he ducked back into the mashed potatoes, and Ellen did, too.

Mrs. Douglas talked about Leona's birth for the rest of the meal, and no one else said much. Leona kept looking at Ellen, and Ellen kept eating, so as not to look at Leona.

It was an uncomfortable ride back to their apartment. Leona looked out the window continuously all the way up Florida Avenue. "I'm sorry about my parents," she said at last, just as Ellen was parking the car.

"What about them?" Ellen said, surprised.

"I'm sorry they're . . . I don't know," said Leona. "Never mind."

"I liked them both," said Ellen. "I really did. God, compared with my mother, they're fabulously sane. I would move in with them in a minute. The food alone would be worth it."

"My mom can cook," admitted Leona.

"Your mom can make heaven sit on a plate," said Ellen, which broke the ice a little. They left the car and walked toward their apartment. Ellen thought to herself, as they walked, something is different, here. She considered it for a moment. Yes, she knew what it was. Leona had declared herself to be in love with Ellen, but Ellen had not declared anything. The balance of the relationship had shifted at that moment. Ellen didn't like it. She had been in more or less the same situation with men, but it hadn't made her feel like this. She felt awkward, unnaturally large, and her hands felt heavy and hard at the ends of her arms. She had never noticed that she was taller than Leona until that moment, or that her boots made such a loud, obnoxious sound on the pavement.

They arrived in the living room of their apartment, and Leona puttered around, removing dead leaves from some freesias that she had put on the blue table that morning. Ellen busied herself also; lowering the blinds over the front window, checking the geranium on the sill to see if the soil was too dry, tucking a yellow, Indian cotton bedspread more firmly over the folded futon that served as their sofa. She had to go to the bathroom, actually, but Leona was between her and it, and she somehow didn't want to cross the room in front of Leona.

Finally, to her relief, Leona went into the kitchen and began preparing tea. Ellen scuttled to the bathroom. Once seated inside, and studying the pattern of the floor tiles between her feet, Ellen decided that she would allow Leona to make a pass at her, if that's what she wanted to do. That is the only way, she told herself, that I am going to know if this is right or not. (I wonder if I should brush my teeth?)

Resolved, Ellen marched out into the other room, but Leona was sitting at the table with a cup of tea, and didn't look all that inclined toward making a pass. She looked, in fact, the way she did when she was contemplating one of the more heinous excesses of global patriarchy: foot binding in China, say, or African clitoridectomy. That look was usually Ellen's cue to prepare herself to hear an eloquent, stinging, verbal assault on the betesticled, but for all Ellen knew, it was Leona's pre-romantic-overture look as well. Ellen poured herself a cup of tea and sat down on the sofa, pretending to be absorbed in the homilies on the Celestial Seasonings tea package.

WE TREAT THIS WORLD OF OURS AS THOUGH WE HAVE A SPARE IN THE TRUNK, she read. True enough.

Leona got up, then, and came over to the sofa and sat down beside Ellen. Not close, but rather about a foot away. Ellen looked at her, at her smooth brown skin, her wild hair, strong nose, full mouth, and shining dark eyes. What an amazing woman she is, Ellen thought to herself. So beautiful, and she knows what she wants. She is so sure.

"Something is going to happen, now," Leona said. "You know what it is, Ellen, and I don't."

"I don't know, either," said Ellen.

"You do," said Leona. She leaned across Ellen, reaching to shut off the lamp that shone brightly on both of them. Ellen could smell the good Leona-smell in her hair, and she marveled at its softness as it brushed her cheek. The light was clicked off, and Leona moved back. The distance between them seemed impassably large.

To move twelve inches into an embrace was a declaration of intent to be in that embrace. I couldn't just pretend that it was an accident, Ellen thought. If I wind up over there, near her, she will know that that is where I have decided to be.

They sat that way, a foot apart, for what seemed like a very long time. The light from a streetlamp filtered in through the branches of the ginkgo tree and through the blinds. It lit Leona's hair from behind. Ellen could not see Leona's face. She could hear Leona breathing, and could smell the sweet hibiscus tea and honey on her breath.

At last Leona, taking hold of Ellen's hands, made her own, declaratory move across the space between them, tilting her head to one side, and kissing Ellen's mouth.

It was a surprisingly agreeable moment.

Being kissed by a woman, Ellen discovered, was very much like being kissed by a man, except that Leona's mouth was softer, with no whiskers to sand away the outer dermal layer of Ellen's chin, and the kiss was gentler, without the determined muscularity that Ellen knew in men's kisses only by its absence now in this, a woman's kiss. Leona's mouth tasted of tea. Her hands, where they held Ellen's own in Ellen's lap, were hot, or else Ellen's hands were very cold. Ellen, allowing herself to be kissed, wondered, in a distracted sort of way, about breasts.

What do we do with our breasts?

Where do they go, when we embrace?

Admittedly, Ellen did not have much in the way of breasts, but nonetheless, there was more squishy tissue on her chest than there would be on a man's. And Leona was fairly "well endowed," as they say. What would happen to all that female flesh when they moved, as they perhaps would feel called upon to do, more completely into each other's arms?

(Maybe I should've researched this first, Ellen thought.)

"What are you thinking about?" said Leona, her mouth still a soft presence against Ellen's, talking against her skin, tickling her.

"Breasts," said Ellen. "I was thinking about breasts."

"So was I," said Leona. "What a coincidence."

"I don't really have much in that department," said Ellen.

"I know, Ellen," said Leona. "I've lived with you for nine months, remember?"

"Oh yes. Well," said Ellen. "I'm sorry about that."

Leona's hands left Ellen's hands, and came to rest on Ellen's knees. Ellen looked down at them: two familiar, brown shapes in the darkness, her friend Leona's hands. A small, V-shaped scar glowed on the knuckle of her right index finger, which Ellen knew to be the souvenir of an encounter with a barbed-wire fence at the farm to which Leona, as an inner-city youngster, had been taken in the first grade. The scar was pale yellow, the same color as Leona's nail beds and palms. Ellen felt Leona kiss her cheek, felt the soft fuzz of Leona's hair brush her ear.

"You're fine," said Leona. "You're wonderful."

I'm not wonderful, Ellen responded, but not out loud.

"Well, where do they go?" she said instead, with a forcefulness that surprised her. "The breasts? I mean, when you embrace a woman, what happens to . . . all that bosom?"

"What do you mean, what happens to it?" said Leona.

"Does it all sort of mush to the side, or what?" said Ellen.

Leona took her hands off Ellen's knees, and sat back on the futon. "Somehow, that isn't what I was hoping that you were thinking about," she said.

"Well, I'm new at this, I don't know all the correct, woman-identified things to think about, yet," said Ellen. "Men never ask what you are thinking about."

Leona snorted. "Men," she said.

"Well, I can't help it," said Ellen. "I can't help it if I am . . . was . . . heterosexual."

"What do you mean, *was*?" said Leona. "It's not that easy to jump the fence, you know."

"I don't know what I am," said Ellen. "I *could* be gay, couldn't I?"

"I don't think you are," said Leona, "and I definitely don't think that I am the right person for you to find out with." She slapped her hands down on her knees the way a judge drops a gavel. The slap was hard enough to make Ellen jump at the sound it made. Leona stood up. She flicked on the overhead light. It was too bright, and Ellen winced in the glare. "You will have to find your own way to heaven, sweet baby."

"I don't understand. I love you, Leona," said Ellen, feeling absurdly mournful. "You are my best friend."

"What are we, six years old now?" said Leona. "Get a grip, Ellen. We aren't talking friend, here. We're talking sex. I am, anyway."

She was stalking over to the coat closet, removing her denim jacket from it, sliding it on over her T-shirt.

"Where are you going?" said Ellen. "Don't you think we should discuss this?"

"Discuss what?" said Leona, "I wanted to make love and you didn't. That's cool. Why chew on it? Just accept it. Accept it as a gift from Jesus." She laughed, sort of, and was gone.

This is what she would say, whenever Ellen tried to bring the subject of that night up again: Just accept it. And spring began to turn itself into summer with the impatience of a southern city climate, and not long after that the lease on the apartment expired, and Ellen found Saul.

Chapter IX

"I think I should marry you," said Saul, early on.

"Marry?" said Ellen.

"Yeah," said Saul. His tone was calm, only the reddening of his ears betrayed this as other than a casual suggestion. "Marry. You know, as in husband and wife, happily ever after. Rings. Community property. Children. The whole enchilada."

"Marry?" said Ellen again, mouth agape.

"Marry, Ellen. Marry. It's a common practice, where I come from. People do it all the time."

Ellen had never even been to a wedding. She only remembered Maude going to one, and all Maude would say about it was that the bride was barefoot, and bowls of rolled joints were handed out to the guests at the reception. "*You* want to marry *me?*" said Ellen, getting it all quite clear in her mind.

"Yes," said Saul firmly. "I do."

"Well, we'll see," said Ellen, but the idea began to seem curiously comfortable. She collected her things, her books, her baggage and her futon mattress, and moved out of the apartment on S Street when the lease she shared with Leona expired in June of that year. She moved into Saul's smaller, shabbier apartment in a semi-ghetto neighborhood north of Adams Morgan. She missed the window, the ginkgo tree, and Leona, but she did, she really did, love Saul.

Leona, for her part, moved into a lesbian group house in Mount Pleasant, which Saul dubbed "Casa Labia."

"A cop!" said Leona, astounded, when she was first told of how Saul made his living. "A poh-leece man?"

"An officer of the law," Ellen corrected her primly.

"Fuzz," said Leona.

This is how Ellen and Saul met: Ellen, normally the most law-abiding of citizens, committed a moving violation.

She had stopped for a red light just where Dupont Circle gives way to Connecticut Avenue, headed downtown. The light was set at a peculiar angle to the street, and Ellen could not quite decide whether it was intended for the traffic in her particular lane or not.

But she did stop, just to be on the safe side. And she did notice the police car behind her, which also stopped, but suddenly, as though (Ellen thought) the driver hadn't quite been expecting to do so. And then (it seemed) a lot of other cars began honking their horns.

Hell, Ellen thought. That red light isn't for me. Or is it? No, it couldn't be. So she drove forward. The squad car also drove forward, with its lights flashing, and a little squawk of the siren in case the message needed reinforcement. Ellen pulled over to the side of the street, her face flushed with contrition.

"Are you just trying to see if I'm awake today, ma'am?" said the police officer, when he arrived at her window.

He was a large white man in mirrored sunglasses. Ellen could see a determined stubble of beard on his jaw. He looked past her into the car, and Ellen was suddenly acutely aware of the mess: the fast-food bags, soda cans, newspapers, battered textbooks, pennies, lint, Juicy Fruit wrappers and other detritus that littered the floor of her old blue Toyota.

"Oh, Officer," she said. "I ran that red light back there,

didn't I? I just got so confused. I'm terribly sorry." (Her own face peered back at her from the left lens of his sunglasses, spread wide by the bend in the glass so that all Ellen could see was a set of tiny, frightened, piggish eyes behind an enormous, rose-colored nose. It was a discouraging image.) "I thought the light must be for the Massachusetts Avenue traffic, not for me, and . . . um . . . I was confused . . ." Ellen tried to remember whether she had had a bath recently. She wondered if she smelled funky.

If she did, the cop betrayed no awareness of it. He took her driver's license and registration, his face impassive.

Ellen berated herself silently, as she was prone to excessive guilt over such matters as a violation of the law, especially in a dirty car, but she did sneak a peek at the cop in the rearview mirror as he walked back to his cruiser. My, my, my, she said to herself. Would you look at that?

The cop is cute.

The dude is fine, as Leona would say (though not about dudes), with a fine, strong back, and a fine, comfortable, masculine walk . . .

Oh, ick, said the feminist Ellen severely, *masculine*? But there it was.

When the cop came back, he had taken off his sunglasses, and he smiled at her as he returned her license and registration, his teeth dazzlingly white in the shadow of his beard.

"It's your lucky day," he said, leaning down to look into her face with eyes that were blue and surprisingly kind. His hand was resting on the windowsill of Ellen's car. "I'm about to go off duty, and I didn't feel like giving another ticket." He looked at her expectantly.

"Oh. Well, thanks *very* much," said Ellen. "That's really nice of you."

"You're welcome," he said, still not removing his hand from the windowsill.

"I won't do it again," said Ellen earnestly. (I'm a good person, really I am. Sir.)

The cop sighed, and straightened up.

"I'm sure you won't," he said. He went back to his patrol car, and Ellen drove off down Connecticut Avenue, humming, and saying my, my, my.

But then it occurred to her, with a force that made her smack her forehead with one hand, that perhaps he had been waiting for her to say something back there when he was smiling at her with those big white teeth. Something like: Gee whiz, Officer, if you are going off duty, maybe we could go have coffee someplace, and you could explain the traffic patterns of the District of Columbia to me in detail. Oh, it would be so helpful, Officer, sir. What did you say your name was, by the way?

What *was* his name?

He must have been wearing a name tag?

Ellen couldn't remember. And she was acutely disappointed.

But then Ellen, remembering the sight of herself reflected in those horrible sunglasses and taking a quick whiff of her own armpit, decided that she must have read the signals wrong (again) and mistaken simple, public-spirited friendliness for romantic interest.

Nevertheless, she haunted Dupont Circle for weeks (freshly showered, and in a clean car) hoping to run across him, and even invented a few non-reasons why she needed to run over to the Third District police station. (For the first time in her life, Ellen had a legally registered bicycle, and knew how to license a dog, should she ever acquire one.)

Saul, meanwhile, had come up with Ellen's (unlisted) phone number, via an unscrupulous use of police computer equipment, but was too shy to call her until at least a month after Ellen had driven through the stop light.

"It's some dude named Saul," Leona announced, having answered the telephone.

"Saul?" said Ellen. "Saul who?" she said into the receiver.

"Um, Saul Shepherd. Officer Shepherd, of Metro Police? I, uh, pulled you over for running a red light a while back. You probably don't remember me, do you?"

"Yes," said Ellen carefully, trying not to sound ecstatic. "I do."

"Well, um, listen. I was thinking, maybe you'd, um, like to go out with me sometime?"

"Go out with you?" said Ellen.

"Yeah, on, um, a date."

"Okay," said Ellen.

"How about now?" said Saul.

"Okay," said Ellen.

"Now?" said Leona, when Ellen got off the telephone.

"Might as well," said Ellen, shrugging.

Saul arrived an hour later, wearing regular clothes: khaki pants and a blue-and-white striped shirt. His hair was wet from showering. His ears turned red when she opened the door to let him in. They walked over to Eighteenth Street for coffee and cheesecake, conversation, and the shy pressure of knees under a little marble tabletop in the garden of the Café Lautrec.

"I'm in love, I think," said Ellen the next morning to Leona over breakfast.

"Big deal," said Leona, having forgotten all about Saul. "Who is she?"

"It's a he," said Ellen.

And Leona said: Oh.

Oh, of course.

Later on, she asked Ellen, with an edge in her voice, what Ellen saw in *this* guy? "He's just another mean white dude, Ellen," she said. "Same old same old."

"He isn't the same old same old," said Ellen. "He is wonderful."

"Huh," said Leona.

"He smells good," said Ellen.

"Yeah, yeah," said Leona.

"He smells sweet, " said Ellen.

"He smells like gun oil," said Leona. "My uncle had a gun, and he smelled liked that. "

"Yes!" said Ellen with enthusiasm. "Gun oil, and leather polish, and cloves."

"I'm sorry I asked," said Leona.

Ellen, having moved in with Saul a mere two months after their first date, found herself becoming a cop's spouse, even before they were married. She developed an ear for sirens, for one thing: and a pain in the pit of her stomach whenever the characteristic yelp of a police car sounded anywhere in her vicinity. She paid increased attention to the local evening news, and less to the national news. Screw Central America, she thought. And who gives a damn about what Congress is up to? Have there been any arrests, have there been any assaults on officers of the law? Special broadcasts ("We interrupt this program to bring you a special report . . . ") were cause for Ellen to stop whatever she was doing, and glue herself to the tube—was it a local situation? A cop gunned down somewhere in the city, the identity of whom could not be released over the air because the next of kin—oh, God, would Martin remember to call her?—had not been notified?

Mere national emergencies, bombing raids over Libya, airplane hijackings, train derailments, troop movements, were cause for relief. Once, when a police officer was shot and wounded somewhere down in Southeast, the terrible fact was that Ellen's first feeling was gratitude: The unidentified officer was female. *It isn't Saul.*

Saul was a big, mean-looking man, with a gun on his hip, but the back of his neck was pale and clean, innocent as a child's throat, and as vulnerable. Whenever she glimpsed this portion of her lover's anatomy, Ellen, the knee-jerk liberal, found herself admonishing Saul to shoot anyone who threatened him in any way. "Better them than you," she said to him. "Better *anyone* than you."

Saul laughed at her worry, and hugged her, and lectured her on the proper uses of deadly force. He would act out various scenarios for her, demonstrate the art of the billy club, or the heavy, "Mag-Lite" flashlight that he carried, and when all else failed, he assured her that he would use his gun if necessary. He showed her how he positioned a suspect in such a way that a flick of Saul's foot could topple him if it looked as if the suspect were going for a weapon.

Saul didn't know how serious Ellen was when she said: Don't fiddle with all of that. Shoot them all. Don't take any chances, just gun the fuckers down.

It was an unfamiliar feeling, this love for a man.

There was sex, of course, and that was fine ("*My,* this is fine," she said to him). Even Ellen's fertility, which past male lovers had considered a disagreeable obstacle to be overcome at all cost (preferably by Ellen alone, in the bathroom, on the pretext of applying more deodorant), was something which could be celebrated and, potentially at least, surrendered to. Sex with Saul made sex sensible, at last.

But the love was the astonishing part for Ellen. Not Saul's love for Ellen, although he did love her, and said so, but hers for him. *I love him,* Ellen would announce to herself at odd moments: while brushing her teeth, writing notes in class, or putting coins into the fare box on the metro bus, *I love him.* It was as though she had suddenly become privy to information that everyone else had possessed all along, like the time when she was six years old, riding the school bus home from school, and she had suddenly understood the answer to the riddle "Which weighs more, a ton of bricks, or a ton of feathers?" Ellen, at twenty-one, said *I love Saul* to herself with the same clean joy with which she had, at six, said *a ton is a ton is a ton!*

She told Saul that she loved him. She sang songs to him at

night in bed, all of the old songs that Grummy liked to sing: "Stardust," "Sentimental Journey," and "You Belong to Me." (He didn't seem to notice that she sang off-key.) She brought him pizza or Chinese take-out for lunch at the station house. (He gave her a tour of the place, and introduced her to a couple of prostitutes that were awaiting processing back in the holding cells.) She brought him an enormous (and probably embarrassing) bouquet of flowers and Martin found them a jar to put the flowers in, as there were (understandably) no vases around. That was the day that Ellen was introduced to Martin. ("And he has *nice* friends!" Ellen said to Leona, who snorted and replied: "Men don't have friends.")

And Ellen talked to Saul.

"That's all you did, on our first date," Saul remembered later. "Talk talk talk. Not that you weren't interesting, of course, but I'd never met a woman who could talk as much as you could, without breathing."

Ellen talked about Georgetown, she talked about Leona. She talked about why the generic pronoun should be changed to the feminine, and why pornography should be banned. She talked about her mother, about Grummy, and about why women should be admitted to the Catholic priesthood— something Ellen felt strongly about, even though she wasn't Catholic.

Saul, for his part, didn't talk too much. "I'm a listener," he said. "We're perfect for each other."

"We complete each other," he told Ellen one summer night over a dinner of macaroni-and-cheese. "I think I should marry you."

"All right," said Ellen, having thought about it.

Maude was against the idea. "Oh, Ellen, but he's a *policeman!*"

"What's wrong with that?" said Ellen aggressively.

"You'll be a *policeman's wife*," said Maude.

"I will *not* be a 'policeman's wife,' mother," Ellen snapped.

"I'll be . . . well, I'm going to be a feminist theologian, one who *happens* to be married to a cop."

Maude decided to try a different tack. "Men in general," she said, "are wretchedly difficult to live with."

"I love Saul," said Ellen.

"It doesn't matter. You'll see. It doesn't take long for any sensible wife to begin asking herself why she bothers with it, anyway. Men always let you down, they abandon ship when you need them most, they leave you for some young thing the moment you sprout a gray hair. Who needs it?

"Believe me, my dear," Maude said, waggling her finger in Ellen's direction. "I know whereof I speak."

"What are you talking about, Mom?" said Ellen. "Dad didn't leave you for a younger woman. He *died.*"

"Yes, but the writing was on the wall. Mark my words, Ellen, there is no point in getting too attached to any one of them. I, for one, won't ever do it again. Incidentally," Maude went on, "whatever happened to that nice girl you used to live with? What was her name? Linda?"

"Leona," said Ellen.

"Why didn't you stick with her?" said Maude.

"Because I fell in love with Saul," said Ellen. It was the simplest explanation.

"Yes, well," said her mother. "I fell in love with Owen Elliot, and look where it got me. Nowhere," she added, in case Ellen didn't get the point.

Which she must have said for effect, Ellen figured, as Maude Elliot was not exactly left nowhere by the passing of her husband. Financially speaking, at least, she was well provided for.

Owen Elliot was a skinny Democrat with a big nose; a native of Frederick, Maryland; a Korean war veteran; a Princeton graduate, and administrative aide to one of Maryland's more illustrious senators. He died in 1968, killed when his car was crushed by a tractor trailer on what was then called route 70-S.

Ellen, at five, was deemed too young to attend her father's funeral. Instead, she was sent to the Macomb Street playground with Grummy, where she spent the afternoon playing at burials. A one-legged Barbie doll was interred, exhumed, and reinterred in the sandbox, while Grummy sat on the wooden rim, her elegant black pumps half-sunken in sand, weeping quietly into a black-gloved hand.

"What has happened to Daddy, now that he is dead?" Ellen asked her.

"He has gone to heaven," said Grummy. "It is pleasant there. He will like it a lot."

"Is it pleasanter than here?" said Ellen. Grummy looked around.

The Macomb Street playground was a good playground, with swings and a roundabout, and climbing equipment. There was a small community building where red balls were kept for games of Maul Ball and Keep Away, and where in the summertime, college students in bell-bottomed trousers taught the neighborhood children to do tie-dye and papier-mâché.

"Even more pleasant than this," said Grummy. Ellen was impressed.

Owen Elliot was buried in Arlington Cemetery. The Marine in charge of the matter forgot to give Maude the folded flag from her husband's coffin, because the moment the coffin had come to rest on the bottom of the grave, Maude tore herself from the arms of Ellen's Aunt Sally, and tried to hurl herself in after it.

Grummy and Ellen heard about this once they had arrived home, having resurrected the one-legged Barbie doll from the last of many graves, and left her perched in the highest tree branch that Grummy could reach.

"She's under sedation now," said Aunt Sally, her lips compressed with disapproval. "It ought to keep her knocked out long enough to let them fill in Owen's grave, for God's sake." Maude had, Sally told Grummy, gotten halfway into the ground before several stalwart Marines had recovered their wits sufficiently to fall out of formation and retrieve her. Maude had kicked at their shins in her rage.

The assembled relatives bundled Maude into one of the waiting vehicles and she was driven home. She missed the playing of "Taps."

"Can you imagine?" Aunt Sally sniffed. She clearly attributed Maude's behavior to a theatrical impulse rather than to any overwhelming grief on Maude's part, and Ellen, a five-year-old cynic, didn't take it too seriously either, at the time.

Grummy took it seriously. She slept all that night with Maude, and for at least two weeks thereafter, and Ellen, after the first night, abandoned her own room to sleep on the rug beside the bed that Maude had shared with Owen Elliot, and now shared with her mother. What Ellen remembered of mourning her father was the tickling of the rug against her cheek, and the croupy, uneven breathing of her mother in unsettled sleep.

"The marriage was in trouble anyway," Maude would later briskly tell Ellen, when Ellen was around eighteen. "If it hadn't ended in one of our deaths, it would have ended in divorce. Perhaps it was better this way. It let you believe in the romance, don't you think?"

"Not with you around, Mom," said Ellen.

"Well, one is better off looking at life with a cool head, as you do. I do envy you, you know, Ellen, starting out in life with an awareness of the importance of reason. I wish I had gone with what my head told me, and not my heart."

Maude did not allow her mourning time to go much beyond the first six months following Owen Elliot's death. At least, the outward signs of distress ceased after that, and Maude took herself off to American University and signed up for courses in English literature. Ellen went to first grade, and Maude finished her bachelor's degree, and then her master's. She finished her Ph.D. just before Ellen graduated from junior high.

Ellen did not really think about the fact that her mother never remarried, and that she never seemed even to date, although she went to a lot of dinner parties as the required complement to the men in her social circle who were either divorced, bachelors or perhaps homosexual. To Ellen, for whom only her father was an appropriate mate for her mother, it seemed natural enough, at least until she was an adult (relatively speaking) and able to think about such matters in slightly different terms.

"Oh, well," said Maude, when Ellen asked her about this. "For some of us, there is only the one, you know. Only one passionate commitment, however misplaced."

"Why misplaced?" said Ellen.

"Well, you know," said Maude vaguely, waving her hand at Ellen as if to shoo the question away. "Men make better escorts than roommates, anyway. If you only see them now and then, it cuts down on the time spent primping, and leaves open a lot more time for other things."

It was hard to imagine that Maude Elliot, who was always perfectly groomed in any case, would need to primp more in order to make herself acceptable to a live-in man, but then Ellen's standards in this area were not her mother's. None-theless, Ellen had come to suspect that no matter how her mother described herself, she was not a very passionate person after all. Ellen suspected this for a long time, right up until a week or so before she married Saul.

On that day, Ellen came unannounced into her mother's house and found Maude on the sofa in the living room, sleeping peacefully, with one of Owen's old shirts tucked in under her nose. She smiled and her face looked young.

Ellen tiptoed out, and sat on the front porch for a long time, allowing her mother her devoted slumber. And married gladly soon thereafter, as if Maude had somehow unconsciously bestowed her blessing.

Do all women smell a lover's shirts when they get lonesome, or was this another genetic trait passed on from Maude to Ellen? Ellen remembered this later, when she found herself smelling one of Saul's shirts on a dark, fretful night when all she could think about was danger, and the nape of Saul's neck. She wondered if her father's smell had lingered in his shirts for fifteen years, enough to be of comfort to his widow, who had loved him so passionately after all.

Chapter X

Onion. What did I do to deserve you?

"He can say the word *hot* now, also *Ma ma* and *Da*!" Ellen wrote to Leona. "He meows when he sees a cat, an animal he has for some reason developed a pint-sized passion for. He is walking already, a fairly early achievement according to the volumes on child development that I consult daily, neurotically, wondering when sentences come, and whether I am doing this right."

"Doing what right?" Saul said.

"Motherhood," said Ellen.

"Just do it," said Saul. "That's all."

"Why is the world so simple for him, Leona? And why must I love this baby so much?"

Even now, as she stood before the mirror after a pre–Bert Potocka shower, Ellen was thinking not about Bert, or about science or the mother thereof, or even about sex, but (almost against her will) about her baby.

Her baby, funny baby, up from a short nap and clad in a baggy diaper, was stomping around, intent on his own missions (empty the waste can, dig in the potted plants, drop pennies and lint through the heating vents). Periodically he would find

Ellen in the bathroom, and greet her with a sort of Hitler salute, and an emphatic "AH!" which Ellen took to mean "Hi." He smiled with his gums and eight small, even, pearl-white teeth, when she said "AH!" back.

I love him. I love my baby.

Ellen contemplated her legs. They were bald, denuded of their customary fur (what Saul referred to as Ellen's Homegrown Knee Socks). Ellen had shaved her legs for Bert Potocka, and they looked pale and skinny and curiously frail. On one of his passes by, Onion stopped to run a plump pink hand down his mother's shin.

"*Huffl?*" he said, looking up at her, worried.

"They don't hurt," said Ellen. "I just took the hair off. God knows why." Onion smiled, satisfied, and waddled off.

What I need, Ellen thought then, looking down at herself, is another operation. Just so that my belly looks symmetrical.

Her appendectomy scar slanted neatly down from the top of her right hip, almost intersecting the irregular, puckered, dark-pink line of the cesarean section. Surely, Ellen thought, there is something that could be removed on the left, so that the scars together make a smile in this face of a torso: tits for eyes, sharp collarbones for eyebrows, and my round navel for a nose. Ellen pulled her shiny new underwear up to cover the cesarean scar.

"You won't even notice it, after a while," Dr. Billington had assured her. "Your bathing suit, even your underpants will cover it." Others at the hospital kept telling her the same thing; the speech was surprisingly uniform, as though all the residents, medical students and nurses had memorized it off a little card the way Saul had to memorize the Miranda warning.

Even as they were gathering over her prone body, lifting her nightgown, pulling off bandages, cutting, scraping at the pink-lipped, grinning wound they had made in her body with their scalpels and hospital-bred bacteria, the medical people babbled on about how concealable the scar would be.

Which Ellen, at the time, had found peculiar.

After all, she had never thought to conceal her appendectomy scar from anyone. On the contrary, she was proud of it, and had, for instance, shown it to Saul on one of their very first dates. (By contrast, it had taken him months to convince her to allow him to look at her breasts in full light.)

But Ellen did hide this scar. It was ugly to her. It looked like failure.

Ellen felt the cramp in her abdomen again. Was it cystitis, or was it time, yet again, to menstruate?

"*Ugh,*" said Ellen.

"*Ugh . . . ,*" Onion echoed.

Postpartum, Ellen's menses had returned as a shocking, gory stain on the bedsheet one morning last month. Ellen had not had a period for over a year and a half—nine months of pregnancy and twelve months of nursing had suppressed them for that long. The nursing had also, presumably, suppressed ovulation. "Oh," said Saul, when he saw the blood. "I guess this means we should start using the diaphragm again." A thought that neither of them greeted with enthusiasm.

(Ellen remembered the doctor at the clinic, during her post-abortion check-up, waving that very diaphragm in her face. "Remember," the doctor said. "Remember that your periods are irregular." [She did not seem to consider this the blessing that Ellen did.] "You can't count on an estimation of ovulation. For you there is *no safe time.*"

"You can say that again," said Ellen.)

This new blood had caught her off guard, of course, and without "feminine protection," so Saul had been dispatched to the drugstore to purchase tampons and pads, while Ellen bled ignominiously into a washcloth.

"I had forgotten how disgusting this is," she said, when Saul returned, laden with pink boxes.

"Nonsense. It's another beautiful part of womanhood."

"It's yucky."

"Not too," said Saul, peeling the backing off the self-adhesive strip of a sanitary napkin and handing the napkin to his wife. "But it is easier, I must admit, to be a man." He made Ellen some raspberry tea and toast.

"You're a very nurturing type, Saul," Ellen told him. "You should have been a mother."

"I'm a cop, and a father," said Saul. "It's the best I can do."

·—·—·—·—·

Martin told Ellen about Saul-the-Cop once, back when Onion was tiny. Ellen had come down with an acute case of mastitis, and, as luck would have it, Saul had been sent to New Jersey to take part in a cop conference on "Blood Spatter Analysis," so Martin had taken it upon himself to look in on Ellen to make sure she was all right. He found her sitting glumly in an extremely untidy apartment with a hot compress on the affected breast and Onion suckling relentlessly at the other.

Martin was a large black man with hair so short you could see his scalp through it, and see the several battle scars that striped his head. He had another scar on his cheekbone, souvenir of an arrest made on a reluctant suspect armed with a knife. Had Ellen opened the apartment door and found Martin on the other side, not knowing who he was, she would have fainted dead away in terror. But despite his fearsome countenance, and despite the fact that every other word he uttered tended to be obscene, Martin, like Saul, was a nurturing type. He took Ellen's temperature (103° F), gave her some Tylenol, sent out for pizza, washed the dishes and put Onion tenderly to bed.

"What is it with you two, you and Saul?" Ellen asked him, as the Tylenol took effect, and the hot fog began to recede from her head. "Why is it that I never knew any nice men until I met Saul, and now I am suddenly surrounded by sweethearts?"

"You were running with the wrong crowd, I guess," said Martin, tidying up the pizza debris. "You should've been with cops."

"Are all cops like you and Saul?"

"No. Most of them are bastards. It's the job, you know? The guys who, excuse me, *the guys and the ladies* who get into this line of work are either shitheads who like to fuck with people, or else they're guys who want to take care of everything, make everything right, you know. That's Saul. He wants everyone to be cool, everything to be okay. He wants to make the world safe for democracy, like Superman."

"And you, too?"

"Yeah," said Martin. "But I gotta admit, I like to fuck with people a little." He thought about it for a minute. "Actually, Saul likes to fuck with people, too. He likes the chase. We all like the chase. It's a high, you know. Half of us, if we weren't cops, and moral dudes, we'd be criminals just for the fucking fun of it." Martin laughed. "You don't know what Saul is like out there, Ellen. He's funny as shit. He doesn't look fast, or mean, but, Jesus, when he's onto somebody, look out. Ol' Saul, he'll be strolling down the street, smiling at everybody, Officer Motherfucking Friendly in person, you know, and something will happen, he'll see some asshole rip somebody off, or spot someone he knows is wanted for something, and suddenly he's coming down on the guy looking like a motherfucking vision from hell."

"*Saul?*" said Ellen, trying to imagine Saul looking like a vision from hell.

"Saul, absolutely. His ears go back, and his eyes get squinty, and I swear to God, he bares his teeth like a dog."

"*Saul?*" said Ellen.

"Absolutely," said Martin. "He's great."

In the bedroom Ellen applied lavender powder to her eyelids and mascara to her eyelashes in front of the mirror above the bureau she shared with Saul. The surface of the bureau was cluttered with items: half a roll of Life Savers, a cracked coffee cup containing pennies, two paper clips, a dozen or so of the fat, blunt bullets that Saul used for target practice, a bent diaper pin, a dusty bottle of sandalwood perfume oil, a nail clipper, some toenails, and a few framed photographs, mostly of Onion.

There was a photo on the bureau of Saul, grinning in his uniform.

Officer Motherfucking Friendly.

Ellen remembered their first date, or was it the second? when Saul bought Ellen a bottle of Orange Crush, and Ellen, after drinking a bit of it, offered him a sip.

"Unless you don't want my germs," she said.

"Oh, but I'm planning to kiss you anyway," said Saul, taking the bottle. Taking a sip. Ears red. "So it wouldn't matter."

Ellen remembered that when Saul did kiss her, she had felt blessed, clean. Saved, even.

"From what?" Leona had asked her.

"From myself," said Ellen.

Onion was scrabbling around under the bed, getting himself covered with dust mice. Periodically he would give a little *coooeee!* and Ellen would answer him: "Yes, my love, I know where you are. I am still out here, waiting for you."

Ellen, dressed in peach satin underwear iced with an inch of white lace, tried and was barely able to picture Bert Potocka's face. She remembered instead the almost olfactory awareness of his interest in her.

"I don't know why," she said to Saul's photograph, out loud.

I am so familiar to Saul. My hair, my blood, my plain eyelids, me. He is so familiar to me. Bert Potocka has peeled up the edge of my separateness.

Onion emerged from under the bed, covered with dust, and held up his round arms to be lifted.

·—·—·—·—·—·

It was so easy, really.

One hot bright day in early August, Ellen, Saul, Martin, and Leona got on the subway and rode downtown to City Hall. They waited for fifteen minutes or so in a waiting room, together with a number of other people waiting for marriage licenses, copies of old wedding certificates, other bureaucratic nuptialia. The other people looked curiously at Ellen and Saul. As a concession to bridalness, Ellen wore a plain white cotton dress for the occasion, with a wreath of pink roses in her hair. Leona wore a robe that she had bought in an imports store on Columbia Road. The robe was bright yellow. She also wore earrings shaped like toucans. She looked very festive. Martin, meanwhile, had insisted on wearing his dress police uniform, complete with white gloves, and he was sweating profusely in the brutal heat. Saul wore khaki pants, a white shirt, and a turquoise tie.

Maude and Grummy arrived. (Saul's relatives all lived down in Georgia, and had been told that they needn't feel obligated to show up.) The ceremony was very brief. With Leona standing to Ellen's right, looking distinctly skeptical, and Martin standing to Saul's left, at attention, Ellen and Saul vowed to love and honor and be true to each other for better or worse, for richer or poorer, in sickness and in health, until they were parted by death. Grummy sang a rousing chorus of "Stormy Weather." Maude daubed gracefully at her eyes with gloved knuckles. Martin coughed a little. Saul and Ellen said "I do" and kissed each other. Saul hugged Ellen so hard he lifted her up off the floor, and the justice of the peace laughed.

"Is that it?" Ellen whispered, into Saul's ear.

"That's it," said Saul. "We're married."

"Oh," said Ellen. She had thought, for some reason, that the justice of the peace had to hit his little podium with a gavel before it was official.

"Did you mean that, about the death part?" said Leona afterwards, *sotto voce,* when the wedding party had repaired to Rock Creek Park for a picnic.

"Of course I meant it," said Ellen.

"Couldn't you have just said: 'Until we are parted' period?"

"Gee," said Ellen. "What a courageous commitment that

would have been: *Hey, babe, I'll stick around until I don't feel like it anymore.* Something like that?"

Leona sighed. They watched Martin, in his uniform pants and undershirt, trying to teach Grummy how to throw a Frisbee. Grummy was wearing Martin's hat.

"*Mira!*" Grummy called to Maude, who sat primly on a picnic table, drinking wine from a plastic glass.

"English, Mummy!" Maude called back. "Speak English!"

"I don't know," said Leona. "It just seems a little too scary for me."

"It seems a little too scary for me, too," Ellen admitted. "But it has been done. I have made a leap of faith."

"And," said Leona, in a sepulchral voice, "there is nothing left for you but to fall. Or fly," she added hastily, when Ellen gave her a wounded look. "You could just fly. You never know."

Maude said later, over a postwedding, postpicnic supper at her house: "Just wait until you have *children.*" She waggled her fork at Ellen, Saul, Martin, Leona and an uncomprehending Grummy, but prettily. "You think that the wedding is the big part, but the really transforming event comes later (although nowadays you never know). When her own child takes its first breath of this world's air, that is when a woman changes utterly."

"Utterly?" said Ellen.

"A woman?" said Saul. "Not a man?"

"And can you choose what you change into?" said Leona. "I'd like to be a poet. Or a dolphin."

"I'd like to make detective," said Martin.

"You will," said Saul to Martin. "Don't worry. I've heard rumors about you. They say it's in the works."

"No, no, no," said Maude impatiently. "You misunderstand completely. Men don't transform, life transforms around them, and they simply adjust. I am telling you that a woman actually changes in her very soul, becomes something completely different than what she was before."

"What if she doesn't like it?" said Ellen.

"Too bad," said Maude. She sat back in her chair, and sipped delicately from a nearly empty glass of wine. "But she will. You will. We do."

· — · — · — · — ·

One night, three or four months after they were married, Ellen read the Song of Solomon aloud to Saul from her battered, annotated copy of the *Revised Standard Bible*.

> *O that you were like a brother to me,*
> *that nursed at my mother's breast!*
> *I would give you spiced wine to drink,*
> *the juice of my pomegranates*
> *O that his left hand were under my head*
> *and that his right hand embraced me!*

"Far out," said Saul. "Now I know why you majored in theology."

"It had its moments," Ellen admitted.

Later that night, Saul woke up and made passionate, half-conscious love to Ellen. This was done without even a halfhearted attempt at birth control, which was not, in and of itself, unusual. Ellen's diaphragm was, at the time, sitting in the bathroom medicine cabinet. It was gathering dust there. It had not been out of its discreet plastic case since a few weeks before their wedding, and although Ellen and Saul did assure each other frequently that it would be more sensible to wait for Ellen to graduate from Georgetown before having a baby, they tended to assure each other of this after yet another bout of unprotected marital relations. They were both, in fact, ambivalent.

"Ambivalent, hell," said Saul later. "I wasn't ambivalent at all. I wanted a kid."

"That isn't what you said at the time," said Ellen.

"I didn't want you to feel pressured," said Saul.

(Anyone with any sense, as Ellen said to Leona, is ambivalent about childbearing. That is why nature makes it relatively easy to conceive.

"For some of us," said Leona.)

"I'm sure we conceived that night," Ellen said to Saul. "When you awoke and leaped upon me in a frenzy of lust, and had your way with me."

"I thought *you* leaped upon *me*," said Saul. "In a frenzy of lust, and had *your* way with *me*."

"I did?" said Ellen.

"Well, you were the one who was ovulating," said Saul. "Isn't that supposed to make you horny?"

"Maybe," said Ellen, now unable to recall who had leaped on whom. It didn't seem to matter. She was pregnant, and Saul, bless him, cried for joy.

He accompanied her to the obstetrician's office for the first visit, and it was there that he found out that this was not her first pregnancy.

Dr. Billington took a complete medical history, with an emphasis, naturally, on gynecological events. "How many times have you been pregnant?" he asked her.

Saul was sitting beside her in Dr. Billington's office. Dr. Billington was sitting behind his desk, writing things down on a form.

"You mean, do I have any other kids?" said Ellen carefully.

"No, I mean: How many confirmed pregnancies, before this one? Births, miscarriages, stillbirths, abortions."

"Uh, one," said Ellen.

"One pregnancy?" said Dr. Billington. "And how did it end?"

"Um, ab . . . abortion," said Ellen, angry with herself, for stammering.

"Was it an early abortion?" said Dr. Billington. "First trimester?"

"Yes," said Ellen. Saul reached across the space that separated them, and put his hand on her arm.

"Any problems?" said Dr. Billington. Ellen could see him writing on her form. Into the space labeled ABORTIONS, he was inscribing a 1.

"No," said Ellen.

"Fine. It shouldn't be anything to worry about now," said Dr. Billington, looking up, all cheer and business. "Let's have a look at you, shall we?"

He seemed surprised when Saul followed them into the examining room. It was a small room, and Saul and Dr. Billington were very large and male within it.

A woman, a nurse, arrived and squeezed in beside Dr. Billington, handing him gloves, the speculum, the K-Y jelly when he asked for it. He poked around inside Ellen's vagina with gloved fingers, and then peered inside with the aid of the speculum and flashlight.

"Yep," he said, addressing Ellen's crotch. "Yep, yep, yep. About eight weeks pregnant, I'd say."

"What are you looking at?" said Saul, fascinated.

"Well, the appearance of the cervix changes with a pregnancy," explained Dr. Billington. "Along with the size and feel of the uterus."

"Can I see?" said Saul to the doctor, and then said it to Ellen. "Do you mind if I look at your cervix?"

"Not at all," said Ellen from the table. "Go right ahead."

"If we had a mirror, you could look, too," said Saul.

The nurse produced a mirror, and everyone took a gander at Ellen's cervix. Ellen found it interesting enough, although she felt silly looking into the mirror with all those people standing over her and looking also. (It seemed unladylike to look for too long.)

Dr. Billington palpated Ellen's breasts, such as they were, and Saul wanted to try that, too, which he did with a professional air. Neither found any abnormalities.

Saul and Dr. Billington had an interesting conversation about what a police officer should do, if called upon to deliver a child. (Keep calm. Support the mother. Be prepared to catch the body, as it emerges swiftly behind the head. Don't cut the cord. Let the baby nurse. Transport to a hospital as soon as possible.)

"Boy, that was great," said Saul, on their way home. "I can't wait to feel it kick." Later, as they lay on their bed together, Saul gathered Ellen in against his chest and asked her about the abortion.

"All right," said Ellen.

All the lights were out, and their bedroom grew dark as the winter afternoon gave way to evening. The streetlamp outside shone through the iron cage over the window, casting strange, geometric shadows across the bed, and across their male and female bodies.

Was it wrong to have an abortion? Ellen wondered.

She would wonder it again, some months later, with what-would-be-Onion fluttering about inside her. Ellen loved the tenderness of this early quickening, when the fetus moved freely, floating, somersaulting, now and then glancing lightly off the walls of its gentle cage.

Hello, hello, my tiny love. Mummy's out here, and how are you?

Alive.

The other fetus, the baby-not-to-be, had been removed too early for quickening, or for any sign that there was life within, other than a mild congestion in Ellen's abdomen, and a queasiness that was either fear or morning sickness.

"What would have happened, had that baby been born?" Ellen asked Saul. "Would it have been all right after all?"

"Maybe," said Saul.

"I wouldn't have found you," Ellen answered.

"Or, maybe you would have."

"But probably not. I wouldn't have been looking for you, nor you for me. But would my life have proceeded, agreeably enough? And if it would have, can I say that I was saving my own life, in some sense?"

"Is that what you thought at the time?"

Yes.

I was resisting life. Not just physical life, the life of the fetus once it was alive (of course it was alive, Ellen said to herself. And of course it died. I won't spare myself knowing that, at least!), but life, the way *life* is, the way that this body I reside in works, what it wants, how it functions.

It was hubris of a wicked sort, wasn't it? To proceed as if the evident unfairness of how reproductive responsibilities have been parceled out merely had to be recognized to be conquered. As if I couldn't become pregnant unless I willed it, that I could, in some ultimate sense, control birth? The abortion . . . God, an ugly word, unspeakable . . . was just one of a series of resistant acts in the ongoing struggle between mind and body. I wish I could say that it was the last of such acts, but I know different. I feel that I shall struggle with this until the day I die. "One can only hope that there need be no more casualties."

"Casualties?" said Saul. "Like who?"

"Oh, I don't know," said Ellen. *Like you, my husband.*

I would have loved the baby. This must be known, too, although (or because) it is painful to know it. Even if it was the product of a less than holy union, mine with Frederick Plimpton, still, the baby would have kicked within, been born, been beautiful, and I would have loved her. Or him. Or it.

I do love him, or her, or it. Even now, as my second pregnancy advances to sacred viability, I do love and miss the first, my ghost-baby, perpetually in limbo, caught forever in the fourth week of gestational existence, a pale being with finger-buds and a tiny spark of a heart. What do I do with that sorrow, anyway? Or with the feeling that I owe someone something. That I paid for my present contentment with someone else's currency?

("Don't be too quick to dispose of your guilt," Maude said once, in another context. "You may need it someday.")

Ellen told Saul about the abortion, and about the long days of bleeding when it was done. She told him how afterwards, even though it had been an early abortion, done when the pregnancy was barely more than cells and blood, her breasts had swelled. They had leaked colostrum, too, as though her breasts knew only that there had been a baby inside, and that it was now outside, in the world, and must therefore be hungry, and in need of nourishment.

Saul was quiet, listening. He stroked her back, kissing her now and then with his warm mouth. His chin, whiskery, scratched her forehead. Ellen cried. She pressed her face into her husband's furry chest, inhaling his clove smell down into her lungs, feeling with her cheek the thud of his stout heart.

"We are having this baby," she said. "This one, in here."

"Yes, we are," said Saul. "And we will love her well. Or him. Whichever."

Ellen felt joy well up inside of her, mixing with sorrow, spreading from her filling womb to her heart, her breasts and limbs, humming in her brain.

"Do you know," said Ellen to Saul in the peace of their bed, "what a miracle you are?"

"I'm not a miracle," said Saul. "I'm just ordinary. This, however," he said, patting her still-flat stomach, "is a miracle. I wonder what sex it is? I guess it doesn't matter. I kind of hope it's a girl. Shall we name it Leona?"

Ah, the baby. The real baby. The one God would not snatch back, in vengeance for the one that Ellen had rejected. Does this mean that you aren't angry with me, after all, for saying no to the first miracle you sent my way? God replied, in Her own way. God sent Onion to be Ellen's firstborn child.

Ellen imagined her own embryo floating, a pale, translucent shrimp busily sprouting fingers and a spine, with that small, bright spark of a heart beating away, not to be interrupted. She liked to think that the first sound the baby heard was not herself speaking, nor even the loving thud of her own, maternal heart, but was, rather, the sound of her placenta, the *shushhh-whirrrr . . . shushhh-whirrr* that had issued forth from Dr. Billington's Dop-Tone amplifier, a sound akin to the ancient sound of the ocean.

How extraordinary, that sex did this, she thought. That something so undignified should result in something so magnificent. She brought her face out of Saul's chest for a moment, to tell him this.

But the miraculous Saul was asleep, smiling. For a long time, Ellen gazed into his closed and quiet face, marveling at the softness sleep imparted to him. In the half-dark, Saul looked beardless, and his eyelashes were long.

Ellen did not sleep. She lay still, thinking about things, with her eyes on Saul.

· — · — · — · —

"What did I do to deserve this?" said Maude, of being female.

· — · — · — · —

Just as Ellen was leaving, the phone rang.

It is Potocka, begging off, Ellen thought.

Or Saul, with knowing suspicion, or worse, unknowing trust.

The phone rang again.

Ellen answered it.

"Hello," said Leona. "It's me."

"Hello!" said Ellen, shifting Onion onto her other hip, and tucking the phone under her jaw. "I was just in the middle of writing you a letter."

"Wow, voo doo," said Leona. "It's raining here. Surprise, surprise. What's the weather like there?"

"Hot," said Ellen.

"Surprise, surprise," said Leona. "Well, so much for the chit-chat. Life sucks."

"Does it suck?" said Ellen. "Why?"

"Oh, I don't know. Are you in a hurry? Do you need to be somewhere?"

Ellen looked at her watch. It was time to go, but on the other hand she wanted to listen to Leona's voice. Possibly for the rest of the afternoon. "I never need to be anywhere," she said.

"Lucky you," said Leona.

"Lucky me," said Ellen. "How is Saffron?" She heard a huff as Leona sighed into the phone.

"We broke up. She wanted more space than Sisterspace afforded her, or something like that. I can't remember what. Something about how she was tired of cooking. Something about how she needed more room. More room! She'd already moved to the other end of Sisterspace, we slept in separate beds. I saw her maybe twice a week, but that wasn't enough space. She moved out, I stayed. That's the way the cookie crumbles."

"I'm sorry," said Ellen.

"Sisterspace isn't the same without her."

"I can imagine."

"And June and Elsbeth parted company, too, after three years. Three years! Elsbeth moved out. She wants children, but June isn't sure. She says children interfere with space. June wants more space. Everyone wants more space."

"I can dig it," said Ellen.

"Elsbeth and Saffron come for dinner every week or so, because lesbians never goddam break up, we just go on being good friends if it kills us. Sometimes it kills me to have Saffron at the table. I'm not good at emotional dinner parties, as you know. And all this talk about space. Emotional space, intellectual space, how space functions in Olga Broumas's poetry, or some godddam thing, blah blah. Space space space. Well, I have too much space, if you want to know the truth," said Leona. "I'm so *depressed*."

"Oh, Leona," said Ellen.

"I want my mommy."

"Don't we all?" said Ellen.

"It's all a big fat crisis. Saffron, my life. My life is a mess. I'm supposed to be writing poetry here, but I am beginning to realize that I'm not a poet. I may, in fact, be a biologist at heart. And what if I'm not a lesbian, after all?"

"What?" said Ellen. "*What?*"

"Well, what if I just made an error, you know? I mean, maybe I should have tried doing the wild thing with someone other than my cousin Bobo? Should I go through life with the wrong sexual identity just because Bobo is a goddam crappy kisser?"

"Uh, I don't know," said Ellen. "But listen, Leona, this is making me very nervous."

"It's making you nervous, that I might not be gay? I thought I made you nervous because I *was* gay."

"Well, that used to make me nervous," said Ellen. "Not any longer."

"Damn. White people sure are funny," said Leona.

"Listen, Leona, in all seriousness, if you weren't gay, I think you'd have had some inkling by now. Y'know? I mean, there you are, out in Oregon, for crying out loud, and it's all very new and strange to you. But I don't think the problem is one of sexual identity. Really."

"Really?" said Leona.

"Absolutely. If you wanted a man, you'd have had one by now. It isn't as though you're timid about this kind of thing."

"This is true. And ugh, I don't want a man. Ugh. Ugh."

"They aren't that bad," Ellen protested.

"Ugh," said Leona again.

"Well, but a man is the only other possibility, isn't it?"

"I guess so," said Leona glumly. "Even if I fucked sheep, they'd be one or the other."

"You're the biologist. But listen, Leona, I think the problem is not one of proclivity but one of context."

"Context," said Leona.

"You need to find the right context," said Ellen.

"You mean, like another relationship?"

"Yes. Like the right relationship. Or the right job. Or both."

"Hah."

"Have faith. Millions of homos can't be wrong. Or any wronger than the rest of us."

"I suppose," said Leona. "But, God! A gay biologist. Is that an oxymoron, or what?"

"Is it? I don't know why. Look at me, for crying out loud. I am a walking, breathing oxymoron, rapidly and inevitably becoming a plain old moron."

"I'd have to go back to grad school," said Leona, "and torture rats. I don't know if Sisterspace is ready for this. I don't know if I am ready for Sisterspace, or space at all. I miss my family, sometimes, and you. I think about you, Ellen. What you have is what a lot of women long for."

"What you have," said Ellen, "a lot of women long for, too."

"I suppose," said Leona dubiously.

"Like me, for instance."

"Yeah, right," said Leona. "Why is that? You've got a context. You've got context out the wahzoo."

"Do I ever," said Ellen. "But is it the right one?"

"Are you and Saul okay? Don't tell me you are having doubts. I couldn't stand it."

"Well, sort of," said Ellen. "But listen, I do sort of have to be somewhere . . . um . . . can I call you back?"

"Okay. Tonight. I have a lot to tell you."

"I have a lot to tell you, too. I love you."

"Yeah, yeah," said Leona, but gladly, and hung up.

Chapter XI

"So," said Potocka, somewhat testily. Ellen wasn't interested in the motorcycle this time, nor even in the most perfunctory version of the wild, unlikely and instantly orgasmic sex they had once engaged in during these dream sequences. Ellen was ready to cut to the chase.

She had been welling up with words all afternoon, even as she buckled Onion into his car seat. He cried—the vinyl padding was hot from the sun, and Ellen could feel the sweat begun to seep out from under the layer of deodorant in her armpits. She was on her way to see the real Bert Potocka, although her destination seemed almost beside the point at this moment. She had sprayed cologne on her throat before walking out the door. It seemed a dutiful gesture, like a toast to some part of herself that she would leave behind that day, although what part, exactly, of herself it would be was anyone's guess.

In the car on the way to her mother's house, Ellen began to converse with the Potocka in her head. She could feel her head nod, and her hands twitched on the steering wheel, longing to gesture. Onion looked out of the window, practicing his "O" sound.

"So, what wisdom would you impart to me, this time?" said Potocka.

"Well," said Ellen, "I was thinking about biological origins. Evolution."

"Darwin?" said Potocka. "Oh, for crying out loud! But we aren't talking about nature here, are we? Aren't we conversing—if I may use the word loosely—on the subject of religion?"

"You're getting pretty snotty," said Ellen, "for a figment of my imagination."

"I won't be a figment for long," said Potocka. "Answer the question."

"Yes, " said Ellen. "We are talking religion. And religion has almost nothing to do with nature, and it certainly isn't natural. Nature is perfect; morally neutral and fully realized at every moment. Human beings are imperfect: We may be relatively moral or relatively immoral, but we are never fully realized. Religion is how we explain and encourage the struggle to become what we are absolutely unable to.

"Take Genesis, for example."

"Genesis, of course," said Potocka, settling down.

"Genesis doesn't explain in biological terms the origins of human relationships, any more than it explains the origins of the organic Earth (although the former would certainly seem to be the primary interest of those who wrote the story!). Certainly it makes no sense at all in evolutionary terms that a romantic sexual relationship between a man and woman should be the model for all human associations and for human bonding.

"Consider this, Potocka . . . and don't think this thought springs only out of maternal chauvinism, either, lest you raise that as an objection . . . because this is what Leona, who knows about these things, once told me: that the real biological model for all human bonding must be the mother with her infant. That Mother-and-Child is the essential unit of human society, and that the instincts required for the viability of this unit are the basis of sociability itself.

"Listen to this: Evolution, with admirable single-mindedness, concerns itself with (or is affected by, I should say) only those attributes that foster an organism's successful reproduction, including, incidentally, those that allow an organism to remain alive long enough to reproduce. (The traits that provide an organism with the capacity to garner sufficient food from her environment, for example, are traits that therefore allow for reproduction. If you don't live, you don't reproduce.) This is what Leona says, and what I shall, in the tradition of Descartes (Oh, Hell, thought Ellen, why not Descartes?), take as my first principle. Additional attributes and traits are tolerated insofar as they either augment successful reproduction, or do not interfere with it. That's another principle. Truly successful reproduction must be defined as not only producing an infant, but also by having that infant reach the age where it can, itself, reproduce.

"Evolution may function at the level of the survival of the individual, but a viable species, not a viable individual, is the result. (Not the intention, since nature is not conscious and does not 'intend.' Still, evolution does act *as if* a viable species were a desired result.) Individuals are necessarily doomed in the short term; whether a species is doomed in the short term or the long term depends on how fruitful its members are before they die. Another important thing to remember about evolution, Leona says, is very simple: What survives, survives. All a gene has to do in order to be replicated through time and space is to confer a characteristic that allows for successful reproduction, even if you and I could imagine another characteristic that might do the job better. That is, by evolution Nature isn't sorting through unlimited possibilities and coming up with the 'best' in any ultimate terms, rather Nature, through the elegant (if brutal) means of natural selection, either transmits or does not transmit the genetic mutations that chance sends along. We might be able to invent more efficient, or certainly more aesthetic, ways of protecting our sinuses from germs and dust than nose hairs, for example, but since nose hairs work, nose hairs are what we have. Remember this.

"So, what relationship, what singular union (in humans as in other mammals) works in this way, which one is crucial to an organism's reproductive success, and therefore to the success of the species in question? Not one between a male and a female—the act of coitus, which is the entire 'relationship' for many mammalian species, including, at times, our own, hardly constitutes a bond or union, even if it provides for conception. Conception, by itself, is not reproductive success."

"Right," said Potocka.

"What is absolutely crucial to the survival of the resulting infant, and therefore crucial to the survival of the species as a whole, is a mother who can recognize her infant, bond with it, feed it and protect it, even to the detriment of her own, individual survival. Her willingness to do this is called maternal instinct in other animals. In human beings, we call it love." A mother loves her infant.

(I found one of your socks in the kitchen last night, Onion, after you'd gone down for the night. It still carried the shape of your foot. I held your little sock to my cheek. I love, O I do love Onion.)

"O . . . O . . . O . . . ," said Onion. (And I love you, Mum.)

"This love is the origin, the reason for all love. It is the reason that love exists at all: because infants need it for life itself. (All mammalian infants need it, even those belonging to species that do not give evidence of requiring other forms of bonding—tigers, for instance.) This bond is the primary material for all human bonds, for all relationships, for society, for civilization."

"Then men must love," said Potocka. "They must." (In Ellen's mind, Potocka's accent tended to take on a peculiar,

Shakespearean tone. Sometimes, without meaning to, she had
him speak in iambic pentameter.)

"Men love," said Ellen, "because nature distributes her
favors generously. Men have nipples on their chests and
women have orgasms, not because either are, strictly speaking, required for reproduction (although both wound up as
two more cards in the stacked deck of greater and lesser
inducements offered to make sex more attractive than it
might otherwise be), but because traits tend to be passed
down to both sexes unless there is some compelling—anti-
reproductive!—reason to make them sex-specific.

"Male animals thus have the capacity for love (which
includes affection, nurturing and friendship) but their expres-
sion of these is somewhat impaired by what I would claim is an
innate (although again, not exclusive) tendency toward
aggression. Can females be aggressive? Certainly, when it is
useful for them to be so. But for reasons which shall be made
obvious, the aggression of females tends to be suppressed in
order that mothers may carry out their vital obligations to love.

"Let us imagine the archetypal primate society in the
childhood of our species. It probably consisted, as many of
our near relatives' societies do, almost entirely of females:
grandmothers, mothers, daughters and infants of both sexes.
Aggression would push most of the adult males to the fringes
of the group because any sensible mammal recognizes that
after adolescence males become dangerously, indiscriminately
aggressive. And because they are this way, one adult male is
permitted to remain within this circle as the so-called
Dominant Male. His function, however, is not to 'provide' for
the females (show me a female chimp who can't yank her own
mango off a branch!) nor to govern, as instincts provide
substantial governance, rather, his function is to defend the
group from the antisocial behavior of the other males lurking
resentfully around the perimeter. The dominant male protects
the women and babies—on whose survival the survival of the

species depends—from males of their own species. He is rewarded with sexual access, in the sense that he is first on the scene, genes at the ready, when nature sends her signal that the moment for assured conception is at hand (that is, the female 'comes into heat'). He is also rewarded, I should add, by inclusion in the group (despite his crabbiness), something he is led to desire by the fact of his having been made a social animal by his inheritance of the gene for love.

"But things took a dramatic turn when these ancestors of ours became human—a turn for the worse, the authors of Genesis would have us believe."

"Genesis? Are we back to Genesis?"

"Of course," said Ellen. "Genesis, you see, is not the beginning. Genesis is the middle.

"Standing up was Genesis.

"Standing up was the Fall. Do you see what I mean?"

"No."

"Well, listen. We are entirely correct to interpret the Fall as sexual and intellectual, but *both,* not one or the other. Imagine this: The first human being (male and female She created them both) hoists herself upright, wrenches her spine straight, tucks in her chin. And becomes human. Poof! An upright body can balance a larger head, an enormous frontal lobe. The human mind is possible. Ah, but standing upright also gave this hominid woman all sorts of reproductive difficulties. Different muscles took the weight of her womb, ligaments strained as gravity exerted itself in new ways. Big brains require big-headed babies, but the pelvic opening could not widen too much, or else locomotion would be impaired, and the muscles slung between the bones would not be able to support the weight of organs pressing down from above. Babies had to be born smaller, frailer, with softer heads to allow them to pass through the barely adequate aperture, and live." (Or not to pass, and die, thought Ellen. As Onion could have

died within, and I without, had it not been for Ol' Billington
and his scalpel. Were it not for this scar. Damn. Damn.)

"More love was required of our mothers, *even more* love,
even more giving and bonding, more care.

"Meanwhile, something else. Imagine that in standing
upright, we somehow lost the estrus, that females no longer
came into heat? Imagine, then, that nature had no way of telling
us that conception was likely, no way to signal us, male and
female, that now was the moment for coitus? What is required,
without estrus?

"A constantly available, constantly horny, sexually aggressive male. Because the only way to ensure that intercourse
results in conception, absent a clear signal of ovulation, is if it
takes place over and over again. Whether the female wants it
or not.

"The anthropology textbook I had at Georgetown referred
to this state of affairs as one in which 'the females gradually
became capable of year-round sexual receptivity, and were
always attractive to males.'

"*Receptivity!* Potocka!

"As though this were a product of a teleological progression
rather than an accident of random evolution, as though this
Russian roulette approach to reproduction were a more
sensible arrangement on the face of it than the surefire
sex-during-estrus variety that preceded it (and that has, I might
add, served other species quite well over millennia). For
receptivity, read vulnerability. There's a clue to the argument,
Potocka.

"(And, by the way, females did not *become* more 'attractive'
to males, rather, males who were not constantly turned on by
the females in the vicinity, whatever their charms, did not
reproduce, and so their lineages terminated.)

"I suppose that nature could have provided for a sexually
aggressive female, but remember her raw materials: males who

are already aggressive, indiscriminate enough to assault their own species, and never incapacitated by pregnancy, and females who, among other things, must look after the babies. Untrammeled aggression in females would be disastrous. In males, it proved to be if not exactly attractive, at least biologically useful. Rape, as my friend Leona would say, became a viable means of genetic survival. The rapists impregnated, the rapists' genes survived. In these terms, rape worked. And so did inequality. It exists because it worked.

"The technological twist on this is that human males also took over the means by which human females fed and sheltered themselves. This is what we now know of as the division of labor: that the means to survival were increasingly appropriated, and traded back to women in exchange for sex, and so was the protection that the Dominant Male had earlier afforded the ladies on instinct alone, free of charge. Here was the deal: I will provide for you, and protect you from the rape of other men, in exchange for your sexual submission to me. Which, of course, meant that female passivity also 'worked.' Nonresistance to male sexual assault (which, without estrus, had lost its context) became a means by which those females properly equipped with the necessary masochism could assure the transmission of their own genes."

"Yikes," said Potocka.

"Yes, yikes. But the human twist on this, Potocka, is that we don't like it. Genesis is proof of this. We aren't so crazy about how evolution, in the strict natural sense of the word, has shaped us, and so with our God and conscious minds, we try to shape ourselves.

"None of us is natural, Potocka. Look at us! We are all perverts, each and every one of us, the straights at least as much as the gays, with our determinedly sterile intercourses, our pornography, our manifold fetishes (including celibacy), not to mention the crimes. Or even the mild perversity of tying our sensual life so closely to our sexuality that we offer sustained physical affection to no one but our lovers (with the temporary exceptions of our children). There is almost nothing about human sexuality, aside from the strict mechanics of the reproductive act, that is 'natural.' While human violence may be an unnatural addition to our sexuality, so is human love (if for no other reason than that it leads us to waste our resources on thwarting Nature's intentions toward our manifestly unfit specimens, hemophiliacs, for example, or the terminally ill). Either would be suicidal for any other animal species, and perhaps both shall be for our own. We haven't been around all that long, remember, and we don't know how it all will pan out in the end.

"But we mustn't be too hard on our poor, perverted selves. It may not be natural, but it is what we call human nature to warp and change ourselves as well as what surrounds us. Consciousness is existentially uncomfortable, and we do want comfort, however ineffectively we may pursue it.

"Eve ate consciousness, and suddenly the world was a difficult place, with violence and love, love and sex, mind and body and human and nature all a great snarl, to be disentangled as best we can, with our poor, enormous human brains.

"The Fall. It makes perfect sense, doesn't it, that Eve should have been the one to fall (or stand) first? That the first split, the confrontation between nature and consciousness should happen first within her? From the first, dread sign of incipient reproductive maturity, the first horrible hair or stain, don't we girls bear, among other things, a constant reluctant witness to the appalling vulnerability of the human body? Don't we learn, far earlier than men do, if they ever do before receiving the final evidence of death, that Nature is not kind? That Nature is terrible and beautiful, but not *nice*? Don't we find out that every natural life involves a little blood, a little pain, or maybe a lot, and death? Eve, in her hubris, did not invent death. She acquired the knowledge of her own living and therefore of death and for this she was punished (appropriately, I suppose) with death's reminder: the multiplied pain she would experience in bringing forth life, along with the capacity to anticipate and remember it.

"Let me tell you," said Ellen.

"The Fall. It was our adolescence, and it repeats itself in human adolescences the world over: in that disgusting, disagreeable time wherein an integrated child disintegrates and fractures before the sudden urgencies of violence and love. But it wasn't uniformly catastrophic, in Eden or in us, this adolescence. It can be overcome. The catastrophe in Eden was what became of violence, the hope is what became of love, and the only access to hope is through the very consciousness that endangers it.

"Think. Think hard.

"If the rapist's genes survived, at least *not only* his survived, and if the masochist was made pregnant, at least it wasn't only she. There was another option open to our male and female ancestors after all, one which made use of a heretofore underutilized ability: the one that allowed men to love women and women to love men. Love, too, was brought forth in service of reproduction, and love, too, worked. If sex became commingled with the giving and receiving of violence, it also, and blessedly, became commingled with love. Perhaps Nature's helpless human infants required more than just enough love, perhaps the genes provided for a surplus, one that has kept the species from more aggression, more infanticide and gynocide and holocaust than it can take. We shall see, I suppose. But one can hope that if there was enough love for societies, in human terms, to form at all, there shall be enough to let us all, male and female, continue to turn our conscious minds toward the good—the human good, which is God—even, or especially, if we know we must inevitably die before we get there.

"Which is what I meant about men speaking the word of God (way back when). If we can't find a yearning toward the good, toward reunion and inclusion in the Bible of men, if we find only the rapist writing there, and the echoing silence of his victim, then we are doomed.

"Fortunately, I believe we can find the lover, too. And the lover is male and female, both and neither.

"For what it's worth.

"What is it worth, Potocka?" Ellen said at last, and guiltily. Even in fantasy, she did have a sense when she had chattered on too long.

Potocka did not reply. Ellen looked around, blinking. The car had parked itself neatly by the curb, and Onion was saying "O . . . O . . . . O . . . " and pointing vigorously at Maude's house, from which Maude herself was emerging, fluffing her hair with a graceful hand and making welcoming little "O's" of her own.

·—·—·—·—·

In the first place, Onion had been two weeks overdue. A sonogram, done at the hospital several days before Ellen went into labor, revealed that he was a large baby, with an enormous head. It also revealed that he was a boy, but Ellen had requested firmly that she not be told what the baby's sex was, and Dr. Billington respected her wishes in this regard. "We want one thing, at least, to be a surprise," as Saul said.

"I'd say we're talking about a good nine pounder," said Dr. Billington, peering at the screen. The sonogram provided a surprisingly clear image of a baby folded to fit into very cramped quarters. Once Dr. Billington pointed out the face, Ellen was astonished at how detailed it was. She watched the baby's eyes blink. A hand floated into view, and swept across the face, as though trying to push the instrument creating the image away, as though the child who would be Onion (or already was) could feel something pressing in from without.

"When do you think I'll go into labor?" said Ellen.

"Well, everything looks fine, and the placenta's in good shape, so we don't really have to worry too much about it. If you go another four or five days or so, we can think about trying some pitocin induction."

"Four or five *days?*" said Ellen.

"Now, now," said Dr. Billington. "It's not that bad, is it?"

It seemed that bad, to Ellen. She was ready for this kid to get the hell out of her body.

Once the morning sickness had abated, almost on the day the second trimester began, Ellen had enjoyed being pregnant. She felt better than she had ever felt in her life: more energetic, more cheerful, more capable. And powerful! I am a mother, she would think. Not just a woman—that neutral, nearly neuter term—but a mother! A bearer of life, an amazon, taking up space with belly and breasts.

Gang way, step back, and watch yourself! I carry a child, and moral authority with it.

For the first time in her life, Ellen felt comfortable defending herself aggressively from the usual annoyances: surly waiters, smokers in nonsmoking sections, and the sorts of men who would make lewd remarks even to a pregnant person. Once, on a downtown bus, a clean-cut white man of her own age in a gray flannel suit bound for some office or another had the temerity to fondle her belly. "Mind, sweetheart?" he said, with a patronizing smile.

"MIND?" Ellen roared, startling other passengers, and causing the bus driver to turn his attention from the traffic on Pennsylvania Avenue. "MIND?!?!?"

"Disgusting pervert," an elderly woman chimed in, raising her three-footed cane threateningly in the man's general direction, and the man reached hastily for the bell cord.

Ellen loved being pregnant, in these middle months. It was only toward the end, in the last month, that she began to feel as though she had been pregnant too long. Forever, in fact, and she wanted to be alone in her own bones again.

The baby performed complicated isometric exercises within her. Little bumps would appear on the otherwise smooth

round of Ellen's belly, sometimes remaining long enough for
Ellen to feel that just under the skin there was a tiny fist or foot
pressing outward. She liked that. But her back ached. It was
impossible to sleep, and she kept Saul awake all night with her
fidgeting, moaning and complaining. Braxton-Hicks contractions would tighten her belly at intervals, practicing for the real
thing, and toward the end each set of these was cause for a race
to the kitchen clock, before the face of which Ellen would
stand, hands on her belly, timing. These contractions never
seemed to come to anything, and each time the tightness in her
muscles loosened and the mild pain faded, Ellen would be
overcome with disappointment and resentment.

Once her due date had come and gone, Ellen began to get
desperate. It is all a sham, she imagined, a great joke that
someone was playing: "I shall always be pregnant," she said to
Saul. "The baby will never come out, and I will always be
enormous, and miserable, and *hot*."

"Let's go get some ice cream," Saul would say. Saul believed
in the power of food. "Chocolate ice cream will stimulate
labor," he would say. "I'm convinced of it. And maybe some
beer, too."

("You're not supposed to drink when you're pregnant,"
Ellen said.

"Hell, that kid is big enough for a bit of beer," said Saul.
"That kid could drink *me* under the table.")

It was dreadfully hot. The week before Onion was born,
Washington was frying in a record heat wave. The air
conditioning managed to lower the temperature inside the
apartment to around 90 degrees, and Ellen spent days indoors,
languishing on the sofa, her swollen feet dunked in a bucket
of lukewarm water. She ventured outdoors only at night, with
Saul. After supper, they would walk together slowly all around
the neighborhood: down Columbia Road past the Burger
King, past the store that sold incense and African music,
the Revolution Bookstore, the Sudz-O-Mat, up Eighteenth

Street past the cafés, the galleries, the Ethiopian restaurants, of which there were three or four on one block. They walked down to Dupont Circle and sat on the grass, listening to reggae on the teenagers' boom boxes, and watching gay men promenade, while old folks played chess and argued. They pointed out babies to each other, and Saul would give Ellen a little hug when she sighed. Once, they walked by the apartment on S Street where Ellen and Leona had lived together. Strangers now occupied their window. Ellen, peering in through the leaves of the ginkgo tree, saw two men kissing by candlelight.

"That's nice, isn't it?" said Ellen. "Love?"

"Sure," said Saul agreeably.

Nice, Ellen thought. And sort of appropriate somehow.

Finally, one set of particularly promising Braxton-Hicks contractions dislodged the plug of mucus from Ellen's cervix: she found it in her underwear, and was tremendously excited.

"It's a sign that it won't be long now, Dr. Billington says," she told Maude over the telephone.

"If you knew what labor was like," said Maude. "You wouldn't be in such a hurry to begin."

That night, a Tuesday night, Ellen woke up at some point, and realized that her contractions hurt. Not dreadfully, but noticeably.

"Well, well, well," she said to herself, and went back to sleep. The next time she woke up, it was six A.M., and she was sitting in a deep, warm lake of water. It took her a moment to realize that the source of this lake was herself, and that more of it was issuing from her in a strong, unstoppable gush.

"Saul! Saul!" she said to him. "My water has broken!"

"Wait, "said Saul. "Wait . . . I'm asleep."

"I can't wait," said Ellen. "Get up. We have to save the mattress."

"EL-len . . . ," Saul whined, rolling over and pulling the pillow over his face, but just then the water began lapping against his lower back, and Saul woke up and realized what was happening. "I'm not ready for this," he said.

Ellen called the doctor.

"Well," he said. "It sounds like today's the day. Just stay put for the time being. Are you having any contractions?"

"Yes," said Ellen. "But they don't hurt much."

"Call me back at nine," said the doctor. "Or when the contractions are five minutes apart."

"Okay," said Ellen.

Shortly, very shortly, thereafter, the contractions began to hurt. They began to hurt a lot. Ellen began panting and breathing, she rocked back and forth, she sang. She stood in the shower, with her face in the spray, saying "*Ow ow ow ow ow ow ow . . .*" Nothing helped. The contractions got stronger.

Saul, meanwhile, had succumbed to a nesting instinct so powerful that he, having forgotten all else, was rushing around with a vacuum cleaner, vacuuming madly. He vacuumed the floor, the rugs, and began on the furniture.

"Saul," Ellen said, standing on a towel, because amniotic fluid was still streaming from her, "this hurts a lot."

Saul vacuumed the sofa, the rocking chair, and the top of the desk, taking up dust, crumbs, and most of a container of paper clips.

"Saul," said Ellen. "The contractions are four minutes apart."

Saul began vacuuming the venetian blinds.

"SAUL!" said Ellen loudly. "SAUL! STOP THAT!"

"What?" said Saul, shutting off the machine. "I can't hear you."

"We have to go to the hospital. The contractions are close together. They hurt."

"I haven't done the walls yet," said Saul, his eyes wide and a little dazed. At which point Ellen burst into tears.

"It hurts so much!" she said. "I didn't know that it would hurt so much!"

They drove to the hospital. Ellen remembered later how the streets had looked: the trees dusty and limp in the heat, the men waiting at the bus stops with their suit jackets slung over their arms, their armpits dark with sweat. Saul kept leaning out the window, waving his badge at vehicles that were not moving along swiftly enough.

"POLICE!" he shouted. "EMERGENCY!"

Ellen leaned her head against the car window, saying *ow ow ow ow ow ow ow*. The contractions continued. They intensified.

Saul parked in an underground parking lot at the hospital, and helped Ellen walk to the elevator which would carry them up to ground level. There was a street person sleeping on the floor of the elevator, a person of indeterminate gender, who peered up at Ellen as they ascended.

"You're having a baby," the person observed, in a gravelly voice.

"Yes," said Saul. "She is."

"I was a baby once," said the person.

"Weren't we all?" said Saul.

"That's what they say, but it's a lie," said the street person, coughing.

They reached ground level, and Ellen and Saul made their way out of the elevator. Just as the doors were closing, the street person said: "That baby has been blessed by Jesus Christ."

"Thank you," said Saul, but the doors were closed by then.

Ellen didn't care if the baby had been blessed at that point. Ellen had forgotten all about the baby. Ellen wanted only for the pain to stop.

Leaving a trail of amniotic puddles, Ellen and Saul made their way into the hospital, through the lobby, down the hallway to a bank of elevators, with frequent stops along that journey during which Ellen pushed her face into Saul's neck and said *ow ow ow ow ow ow*.

Several elevators came and went while Ellen was engaged in

this ritual, with people aboard looking irritated, or understanding, depending on whether or not they could figure out
the cause of her behavior. At last an elevator arrived between
contractions, and Ellen and Saul shuffled aboard. A tiny,
nut-brown man in a green uniform was the only other
passenger on this car. He turned to Ellen and said, "*Es un
chico, no?*"

"*No sé,*" said Saul, who understood more Spanish than
Ellen did.

"*Sí, digo es un chico.*"

"What is he saying?" said Ellen.

"He says the baby is a boy," said Saul.

"*Yo sé. Mira. Es un chico.*"

"Oh," said Ellen. *Ow ow ow ow ow ow ow.*

What baby?

They arrived on the seventh floor. A sign, pointing to the
right, said Maternity Suite.

"Here we are," said Saul, leading Ellen through a pair of
swinging doors. A nurse greeted Ellen by placing one hand on
the top of her stomach. "My goodness, these are strong
contractions!" she said.

"You're telling me," said Ellen.

"Do you feel any urge to push?" said the nurse.

"No," said Ellen.

"Well, holler if you do. I'd say you're pretty close to
delivery."

"Oh, good," said Ellen. "So this is as bad as it gets." *Ow ow
ow ow ow.*

That was around ten o'clock in the morning.

At eleven forty-five that night, the decision was made that
Ellen would have to be delivered by cesarean section. And
Ellen was glad.

This is what she remembered with such shame afterwards:
that when the nurse came in and told her that Dr. Billington
had decided to do a cesarean, and that Ellen had only half an

hour to "make progress" before the decision would go into effect, Ellen said, *"Half an hour? Do it now!"*

She had been in labor for over seventeen hours, but it seemed longer. The hours themselves merged into one long moment of contractions, with what seemed like seconds separating the pains from one another. Saul was there, of course, beside her bed, holding her face, talking her through each contraction, escorting her to the bathroom and staying with her while she peed—something that, for some reason, also made her throw up, which she did into a garbage pail beside the toilet. "It hurts so *much,*" Ellen said to Saul.

"I know," he said.

"Just when I think I can't take any more," said Ellen, "it gets worse."

"I know. I'm sorry," said Saul. "But you're doing really well, Ellen. You're doing a great job."

Ellen threw up. Then she said:

"Who set this up? This sex business? Who arranged it?"

"Not me," said Saul. "God, not me."

His face was gray, and his eyes never left her.

Ellen crouched on the narrow bed with Saul in front of her, she pushed her face into his stomach, smelling his clove smell through the green cloth shirt they had given him to wear. His hip smelled like leather polish and gun oil. His hands were on her back, on her head, on her face.

"You're doing a great job," he kept saying. He watched the busy line on the monitor scratch the signs of an impending contraction: "Here comes another one. You can do it. Hang in there. *I love you.*"

She also remembered the nurses, they were kind and close by, they talked to her and laid their soft hands on her.

"Have you done this?" she asked one of them, at some point.

"Yes," the nurse answered. "Three times!"

"Oh, my God," said Ellen, as she felt the next contraction begin to build.

"It's worth it," said the nurse, as Ellen vanished into the pain. "The baby, I mean. I promise you, it's worth it."

Ellen tried hard to imagine the baby—the baby, that is, whose life required this struggle of her, but the baby, if there was a baby, seemed unrelated to the matter at hand.

What did I do to deserve this? I'm not going to die, am I?

"You're doing fine," they said. "Just relax."

She asked for relief; drugs, that is, of any kind. She begged for drugs, in fact. She was sitting up on the bed, dressed in a johnny gown, with Dr. Billington, two nurses, and Saul standing in a solemn semicircle around the foot of the bed. She asked for something, anything, speaking quickly so as to get her point across before the next contraction wrapped itself around her, and rendered speech impossible.

"I want drugs," she said. "I know I'm not brave, I know I'm not. I'm sorry. Just please give me something."

They did not look as though they felt generous about this. Not even Saul. He looked into his hands.

"Please," said Ellen. "I must insist. Please."

It seemed to her that they were judges, with their serious faces, looking at her over the thin lines of their mouths, it seemed that they were weighing her request against her own worth: Had she suffered enough to deserve relief?

In fact, what they were weighing, as Saul would later tell her, was whether the contractions were having any effect at all upon the descent of a baby who had, by dint of not bending his neck at the appropriate moment, managed to wedge the largest possible circumference of his unusually large head into her pelvic bones. They were considering whether those contractions would be impaired by medication. They were considering cesarean section.

Ellen probably would have picked up on the problem, had she been able to pay attention to what the nurses said when they examined her. She remembered, later, hearing one nurse tell Dr. Billington that she could feel, through Ellen's dilated cervix, the baby's anterior fontanel—the soft spot, in other words, at the front-center of a baby's head. A bad sign.

"Hum," said Dr. Billington at the time, and ordered that Ellen be hooked up to an intravenous drip of Demerol. It did not remove the pain altogether, but it made it seem a little more distant, like the echo of a scream rather than the scream itself. Ellen labored on.

Finally, the nurse announced that Dr. Billington was preparing himself for surgery. "Let's try squatting, and see if you can make any progress at all," she said. "He wants to do a cesarean. We have half an hour to make some progress."

Half an hour? Do it now.

But Ellen did crouch on the floor, between Saul's knees, facing outward, with the nurse scrunched down in front of her, keeping an eye on things, and Ellen pushed. Oh, how she pushed! When a contraction began, she fought it with her pushing, growling deep in her chest, with Saul rubbing her shoulders the way a manager rubs his boxer down in the corner of the ring. *I'm giving it the old college try,* Ellen kept thinking, over and over. *I'm giving it the old college try.* But the old college try proved no more efficacious than anything else they had tried: Onion was not coming out.

Ellen was never gladder to see anyone in her life than she was to see the anesthesiologist, a slight Chinese woman with a tentative smile who arrived at midnight.

"You won't knock her out all the way, will you?" said Saul, standing, for some reason, between the doctors and his wife. "I don't want you to knock her out all the way."

"We use an epidural anesthesia," said the anesthesiologist, edging around him. "She'll still be awake."

"And can I be with her, when you take the baby out?"

"Of course," said Dr. Billington heartily, patting Saul on the back. "We need you there. Ellen needs you there, isn't that right, Ellen?"

"Yes," said Ellen. "I want to be with Saul."

So they sat her up on the side of the bed, with Ellen's head resting on Saul's flat belly and her arms around his waist. The anesthesiologist knelt on the mattress behind her.

"Try to hold very still, even if a contraction comes, okay?" she said to Ellen. "It will be the last one you feel, in any case."

"Okay," said Ellen. The next contraction came, shaking at her, and she struggled to hold herself still. "*Ow ow ow ow ow!*" she said.

"It won't be long now," said Dr. Billington. Ellen lay down on the bed. The contraction faded. And then, miraculously, there was silence below her ribs: the drug spread its coolness from her sternum to her toes, and Ellen, watching her belly contract itself, feeling nothing, laughed. Saul, seeing the pain seep out of her face, laughed, too.

Several orderlies came in, they rolled Ellen, bed and all, out of the labor room and down the hall to surgery. On their way down, they passed another labor room, and Ellen heard a woman screaming.

"I'm glad that isn't you," said Saul.

"Hey!" said Ellen, then. "*Hey!* I'm going to have the baby! Saul, we're going to see the baby!"

"Yes," said Dr. Billington, as they arrived in the operating room. "In about ten minutes, you'll see your baby."

Which they did.

Chapter XII

What was Ellen going to do with Onion while she went to meet Bert Potocka? It was a question she had pondered, and her incapacity for answering it had, for a time, seemed like a subconscious way of avoiding the meeting altogether. Then, fortunately or unfortunately, depending on your point of view, the obvious solution suggested itself: Maude called Ellen on the telephone and allowed as how she would like to spend some time with Onion. *Just* Onion.

"You've been very selfish about that baby, Ellen," her mother told her. "You know how much I adore children, you might have offered him to me, if only for an hour or so."

"I'll tell you what," Ellen said, her heart pounding wildly. "I'll let you have the little cuss for an entire afternoon, what do you think about that?"

"That would be very nice. Tuesday would be particularly good, as Grummy will be here, then. She's not well, you know."

"I know," said Ellen.

"And she is fond of Onion. It would do her good to see him. What's the matter with your voice?" said Maude. "You sound a little breathless."

"It's nerves," said Ellen. "Just maternal nerves. You do remember how to look after little babies, don't you, Mom?"

"Of course I do," said her mother, insulted. "But he's not a *little* baby anyway. He's over a year old, and you, my dear, are not a new mother anymore. It's quite time you realized it."

"I'm doing my best, Mom," said Ellen.

The breathlessness *was* new-mother nerves, in part. Ellen was not good at sharing Onion, and had never left him alone with anyone, other than Saul, of course, and even then it was only for the amount of time required for a quick trip to the grocery store or post office. But Ellen was also asthmatically aware that an afternoon with Bert Potocka was hers for the taking. If I want it, she thought. If I do.

He's probably forgotten all about me, she assured herself, dialing the number Potocka had given her. He had not forgotten her. When he answered the phone, Ellen told him that she had Tuesday afternoon free, if he would like for her to take him up on his offer of . . . well, whatever it was he had offered. "Would you still like to see me?" she asked him. She sounded so businesslike to her own ears. (*Tuesday at one? Very well. And, Professor Potocka, will you be drinking Grand Marnier from my sacral dimples?*) He was pleased to hear from her, and sweetly awkward about it, too.

"Of course," he said. "I would be . . . Well. So happy. But call me Bert."

"Uh . . . Bert," said Ellen.

"Wonderful," said Potocka, and instructed her to meet him at a certain restaurant at one o'clock on Tuesday.

So Ellen, with an aching heart, took leave of her beloved son for the afternoon, abandoning him to the tender mercies of Maude and Grummy. Grummy appropriated him at once. When Ellen left, Grummy was happily piloting a toy truck around the floor with him saying: "*Mira, chico, el tráfico hoy es muy mal! Vroooooommmm!*" and Maude was standing over them, saying, "English, Mummy, *English!*"

"He'll speak Spanish by the time I get back," Ellen said.

"Not if I can help it," said Maude grimly.

Potocka's choice of restaurant was on Connecticut Avenue, not far from Macomb Street. Ellen left the Toyota parked in front of her mother's house, and walked along through the heat slowly. She passed the playground where she had played as a child, and thought about taking Onion there, thought about how he would see, through his eyes, what she had seen through hers, and from the same vantage point. The same sandbox where Ellen and Grummy had awaited the end of her father's burial day was there. One small, black child played with a Tonka backhoe in the sand. A woman, probably the child's mother, sat reading on a bench nearby. She looked up when Ellen went by, and Ellen waved. The woman waved back.

I miss Leona so much, Ellen thought to herself.

Just as Ellen reached Connecticut Avenue, she had a terrible thought: Saul was going to die. He would be killed, right that afternoon, just as Ellen wrapped up her summation of Rosemary Reuther's interpretation of Genesis, and moved into the alien arms of Bert Potocka. Or else, maybe he was already dead, or dying in some hospital room somewhere in the city, with Martin frantically calling the apartment, trying to reach her in time . . .

Stop being so melodramatic, Ellen said to herself fiercely, but she did, nonetheless, stop at a telephone booth and call the Third District HQ.

"Shepherd?" said the sergeant, when he answered the phone. "Yeah, he's fine. He's right here. Hey, Shepherd, it's your ewe, man. Get it?" The sergeant chortled fatly into her ear.

"Hi, Ellen," said Saul, when he got on the phone. "Good thing you caught me, I was just going out."

"Something important?" said Ellen.

"Nah. A bank guy down on the circle has a hair up his ass because some poor homeless bastard with a sense of humor took a piss in the automatic teller machine. 'He youry-nated right in the money slot! *Right* in the *mon*ey slot!' " Saul mimicked the banker, and Ellen could hear Martin howling in the background. "Martin's about to die laughing. Hah! So I'm supposed to go down there with a fucking paper towel and make everybody happy. What a job. But it'll keep. What are you up to? Is Onion okay?"

"Onion's fine. He's with my mother."

"Really? That's great!"

"Why is it great?" said Ellen.

"Well, because if he's with your mother, it means you are alone, right?" said Saul. (Right. For the time being, thought Ellen.) "You've been getting a little crazy lately, El, if you don't mind my saying so, and I think you need to get away from Onion for a while."

"Oh," said Ellen.

"Don't you?"

"Yes, I do," said Ellen.

"You should do it more often. You could leave Onion with me. I mean, for a whole day, if you wanted to. I could take care of him. Hell, I'd *love* to take care of him. All by myself. Father and son. We could take a cruiser down to Anacostia, you know? Blow the siren and see who runs? That's always a blast."

Ellen had a sudden vision of Saul holding Onion. She could see Onion's tiny hand splayed out against the vast expanse of his father's shoulder, the wide, hard, hairy beam of his father's arm beneath Onion's small, dimpled bottom. She saw Onion kiss his father's face, a kiss so sweet it brought tears to Saul's eyes.

"Or you could take him to the zoo," said Ellen. "But you might not like it. Mothering, I mean."

"Do you like it?" said Saul.

"Of course," said Ellen, without thinking.

"But you are unhappy," said Saul. "Lately, anyway."

"Yes," said Ellen. "Sort of. Or confused."

"Do you know why?" asked Saul.

"No," said Ellen. "But I'm working on it."

"Uhuh," said Saul.

"What does that mean?"

"Nothing. But if you want my two cents while you figure this thing out, I think what you really need is to go back to school."

"You do?" said Ellen.

"Yes. You need to have access to some smart people."

"I have you," said Ellen. "You're smart."

"About some things," said Saul. "But I'm not enough. And I don't know enough about the stuff you like to think about to give you any kind of a decent conversation, you know?"

Ellen saw the back of Saul's neck, clean and pale as a child's throat.

"Am I enough for you?"

"Yes," said Saul. "But I have work. I have work and then I have you and Onion. Sour and sweet, you know? It all balances out."

"Are you happy?" said Ellen. "With me?"

"Yeah," said Saul. "I am."

"Oh," said Ellen. "And you'd like to see more of Onion? I don't know if I could bear to leave him for too long, even with you."

"Oh, *Jesus,* Ellen," said Saul.

"I know, I know," said Ellen. "Everyone is getting tired of me, even the baby. I'm trying my hardest to grow up, Saul. I really am."

"Take your time, sweetheart," said Saul. "We can work it all out."

"I hope," said Ellen.

"No big deal," said Saul. "I love you."

"I love you, too," said Ellen, but Saul had already hung up.

·—·—·—·—·

The operating room was still in the process of being prepared for surgery when Ellen was wheeled in. Nurses, technicians and assorted others rushed around with bags of I.V. fluid, stacks of green sterile cloths, trays of instruments. Ellen, with her lower half paralyzed and floppy, a dead weight, was hoisted from the stretcher onto the operating table. A mirror overhead revealed a naked stranger with an enormous belly and a maniacal grin—herself, laid out below. The anesthesiologist took her arms and stretched them out to either side, resting them on little shelves apparently designed for the purpose. They were draped with tubes, and blood pressure cuffs. Ellen made a reference to her position which was, she thought, particularly interesting in a Catholic hospital. No one stopped to discuss this with her.

Ellen looked around for Saul. "Where's Saul?" she asked the green-clad throng. "Where's my husband?"

"Suiting up," said a nurse, as she draped a cloth across a bar, just in front of Ellen's face, so that Ellen couldn't watch the operation. "He needs to wear the same clothes that we do, mask and all." Sure enough, in a matter of minutes Saul arrived in surgical scrubs, his blue eyes bright above the green line of his mask.

"Hi," he said, taking a seat beside Ellen's head.

"Don't I look like Christ on the Cross?"

"Not really," said Saul. "And it's just as well."

"All here?" said Dr. Billington. Yes. The operation began. And was over, in minutes.

First, the doctor and assembled minions laughed: "*Ahhh, look at the size of the kid's head!*" they said to one another.

Then Ellen caught a glimpse of a bloody, wet creature lifted briefly above the screen in front of her, a creature that was instantly taken somewhere off to one side, out of sight. She heard it yowl its first greeting to the world, to this strange, strange world of lights and green figures wielding knives, of plastic hands and of one woman's crazy laughter.

She turned her head, turned, and her eyes found Saul's face, saw the tears running out of his blue eyes, staining the edge of his mask, saw that he was smiling so hard the mask was pulled taut across his cheekbones.

"It's a boy," said Saul. A boy.

A boy. The baby is a boy, the baby is.

Is there anything that comes close to this, in all the wonders of this world: the moment when you know that your child is born, that your child is, that a child has come from you, is of you, and is?

Ellen heard the baby yowl, caught her glimpse of him as he was lifted above the screen between them, saw her blood on him.

Annnhhhhhhh! he said. *Annnnnhhhhh!*

Things happened quickly after that. Saul, having kissed his wife, and kissed her again, took his abler body over to the table where assembled experts thumped his baby's chest to clear it of fluid. Saul was ready when his son was wrapped in towels and handed over.

Saul brought the baby to Ellen, and showed her her son's new face, but someone had given Ellen morphine by that time, and she would not later remember what the face had looked like.

Then Saul and one of the nurses took the baby to the nursery for testing and evaluation, and Ellen remained behind in the operating room, singing to herself, and being sewn up. ("I saw your uterus," Saul would later tell her. "Just before I left, they took it out, and laid it on your belly, and sewed it up. It looked like a purple Oven-Stuffer roaster.")

Ellen sang:

> *Sometimes I wonder why I spend*
> *the lonely nights . . .*
> *Sometimes I wonder why I spend*
> *the lonely nights . . .*
> *Sometimes I wonder why I spend*
> *the lonely nights . . .*

as they showed her her placenta, which looked like a large cow's liver.

Ellen was taken to the recovery room, where she remained more or less alone for what seemed a very long time. The morphine began to wear off, which was just as well, as the nurses monitoring the recovery room were getting tired of Ellen's singing. ("Dreeeaming of a song . . .") The spinal anesthesia was also beginning to wear off. It was nearly dawn, on an August morning. Ellen was a mother.

If God is a woman, she thought to herself, then creation is birth. And birth is part of creation, our link to God via blood, via earth, via a long electric umbilicus that travels back through our mothers, a strand through pearls.

They had whisked her child away from her, and Ellen had not seen him, other than that brief, drugged glimpse from the operating table. Various nurses had stopped by her bed to tell her that the baby was fine, very large, and beautiful.

"Your husband," said one of them, "is the cutest thing I ever saw!"

"Oh?" said Ellen. "Why is that?"

"He's dancing," said the nurse. "He's out in the hallway now, moonwalking with a big black guy, and a teeny-weeny Spanish woman."

"Is my mom out there?" Ellen asked.

"Yes. Do you want to see her?"

"Yes," said Ellen. But where was her baby? When would they stop dancing, and bring him to her?

"Oh, very soon," said the nurse. "We're still warming him up. But we'll bring him in in just a minute. We do want you to bond, after all."

"Well, I'd sort of like to bond, too," said Ellen. "Couldn't he warm up in here, with me? I'm a very warm person. Besides, I want to nurse him."

"Now, dear, be patient! You waited nine months . . . "

"Several years," said Ellen.

" . . . what's another five minutes?"

Eternity, that's what. Grummy appeared before Saul did, striding in as if she owned the place, wearing a bright red hat which spread a round brim over her head and humpy back, and carrying a large bouquet of black-eyed Susans.

"*Mamacita!*" she said, when she caught sight of Ellen. "*Mamacita!*"

"English, Mummy!" called Maude, from the hallway.

"Hello, Grummy," said Ellen. "*Qué pasa?*"

"*Pronto lo sabremos,*" said Grummy. "*Esperare aqui hasta que llegue el policía.*"

"Police?" said Ellen. "Saul, you mean."

"*Sí, Saul, y Martin.*"

"They are still dancing?" said Ellen.

Just then, Saul poked his head around the recovery room door.

"Hey, Ellen," he said. "Wanna see what I've got?"

"Yes," said Ellen. Saul came in, still in his surgical scrubs, his beard black against his pale face, white teeth, all that smile. He carried a bundle of blue blankets from which issued a small but nevertheless emphatic cry.

"Your son wants Mommy," said Saul.

Ellen held out her hands. It took a long time for Saul to cross the room. Finally he, her husband, put their child into Ellen's arms.

How to describe it? That the baby is a comfortable weight in your arms, that he is turning his confused face to yours, that he is looking into your eyes with his new, wet eyes, here you are: *My mother. Here you are.* Ellen touched his soft face with her finger, touched his ears, still slightly crusted with her blood, she palmed his bald head and kissed him.

That he is vulnerable and does not know it, and that this is terrible and beautiful at once to behold. Ellen cried, and peeled back the layered blankets so that she could count his fingers, count his toes, confirm his sex, confirm his wholeness and his life. He was so beautiful. He was so *beautiful.*

The baby mumbled at the air with his mouth, and squeaked.

"What does he want?" said Ellen to Grummy.

"*La leche*," said Grummy, pointing at Ellen's chest.

"He wants to eat," said Saul.

So Ellen, a little awkwardly, found her breast beneath the sheets and tubes that still entwined her, and brought her son's mouth to her nipple, and he, after a moment's confusion, suckled on. There was an unfamiliar, but not objectionable, ache in her breast as his nourishment made itself available. *Oh!*

Maude came in, shyly, as if she weren't sure she belonged there.

"Hi, Mom," said Ellen. "Look, he's eating."

"Hello, darling. How are you?"

"It was awful, Mom. The labor, it was really awful."

"Yes, I know," said Maude. "I know it was awful. But the baby, Ellen, isn't he beautiful? I was hoping for a boy. Hoping for a beautiful boy. Saul says you are going to name him after your father."

"We are?" said Ellen.

"If that's okay," said Saul. "I mean, I know we didn't discuss any boys' names or anything, but I kind of like the name Owen."

"Owen," said Ellen. "Yes. That is a good name. Owen Elliot Shepherd. After my dad."

"*Ahora todos bailan más que nunca*," Grummy observed.

"I'd better take her home," said Maude. "She's had a long night of it. Come on, Mum. We'll come back in the morning."

"*Mañana?*" said Grummy.

Maude sighed. "Tomorrow, Mum. Tomorrow."

Grummy followed Maude. She turned, after Maude had gone out, and stood for a moment in the doorway, looking back at them.

"I am old," she said, in English. "I am old, now." They could not clearly see her face, but her voice did not sound sad.

"I love you, Grummy," said Ellen.

"I love you, too, Maude," said Grummy.

"Ellen," said Ellen.

"Yes," said Grummy.

It was the last time that anyone would hear her speak English.

Ellen and Saul and Onion dozed until morning there, in the recovery room, with their bodies as close together as they could be, given the various tubes and needles, Ellen's tingling legs, and the wound, stapled shut. Ellen and Onion lay belly to belly, breast to mouth. Saul wrapped himself around the outside of this near-unit, his broad back between his wife and son, and the door, and the world.

"We're a family now," he said, before he went to sleep. "What a *trip*."

The nurses appeared to have forgotten all about Ellen, her new baby and her husband. No one returned to Ellen's bedside to fiddle with her catheter, or take her blood pressure, or to remove her baby from her arms again, or to take Saul from her presence. No other patients were brought in. It must have been a slow day for cesareans.

Chapter XIII

The Place of Peace Restaurant, at which Ellen met Bert
Potocka, served miscellaneous vegetarian and Eastern fare,
and was overpriced. The decor was all pale wood and mirrors,
hung lavishly with gilt-framed black-and-white photographs of
a creepy, black-eyed man in a loincloth doing *zazen* on a prayer
mat: the leader of the cult that operated the place, Ellen
guessed. The waiters were WASPs with soft voices and white
turbans, but the kitchen help was all Guatemalan.

"Illegals," as Saul had once told Ellen, as they walked by on
one of their prenatal rambles. "They pay them shit for wages,
too, and the Guats can't complain. Poor suckers. Immigration
does a raid there now and then, and the guy who owns the joint
pretends that he's from Bangladesh or someplace, and that he
doesn't speak enough English to say 'show me your green card,
amigo.' Place of Peace my ass."

I think, Ellen said to herself, crossing the threshold of the
Place of Peace and pausing to search the room for Bert
Potocka, that this restaurant is, as Leona would say, *politically
incorrect.*

But then, so am I.

She looked around the restaurant and saw no one she knew, to her relief. There was one table near the door occupied by a large, uniformly plump family, tourists identifiable by their cameras and armloads of panda paraphernalia from the National Zoo. The children giggled furtively at the pictures of the half-naked guru. The parents raised their eyebrows at each other at the adventure of eating lunch in such an exotic place. The mother took a snapshot of the waiter.

I wish I could have lunch with them, Ellen thought.

But Potocka was waiting for her at the far end. He was rising slowly from a corner table, with his eyes on her. He had long legs, and his hands were in his pockets. He was smiling at her.

It was a shy smile, and sexy enough to make Ellen stumble slightly over some invisible impediment. Funny, she thought to herself, walking toward him. You weren't this handsome, Potocka, the last time I saw you. Or, God knows, in my dreams of you.

"Um, hello," said Ellen, when she got near enough for her suddenly squeaky voice to reach his ears.

"Hello, Ellen," he said. "I am so glad to see you."

"Um," said Ellen. "You are?"

And you didn't have such a delicious voice, either. Are you doing it on purpose? If you had talked like that in my imaginings, I might have let you speak more often. Ha ha.

"I was afraid you had changed your mind. You look beautiful," he continued quickly. "Beautiful, in that costume. Such beautiful eyes."

"Um," said Ellen, thinking of the mascara. "Thank you very much."

"Sit. Sit down here, beside me," said Potocka, withdrawing one hand from his trouser pocket to pull a chair out from under the table. Ellen slid into it, brushing against him, feeling the mild shock of contact with him. He was as urgent in his body as Onion was when it was time to nurse and to Ellen, whose instincts were rusty but still serviceable, the urgency was palpable. *I remember that,* she thought. *Ah yes! I remember!*

They sat in silence for a few minutes. Ellen studied the paisley printed tablecloth, and Potocka studied Ellen surreptitiously from behind his glasses.

"So," he said, after this pause, pulling a package of thin, square-shaped cigars from his shirt pocket. "How is the baby?"

"The baby?" said Ellen, watching Potocka tap a cigar on the table, wondering if this was, in fact, a cheroot. "Oh, Onion, you mean . . . he's fine. Fine. I left him at home, of course. Or rather, with my mother. I've never done it before, since he was born. I guess I'm neurotic about it, even now, after all this time . . . "

"He is a nice baby," Potocka said. He put a cheroot between his lips and lit it. He inhaled smoke. "Have you ever been to this restaurant? I am told it is good." He exhaled, allowing the smoke to drift from his mouth up to where he could suck it back in through his nostrils.

Ellen contemplated telling him about the exploited illegal aliens in the kitchen, but decided that it might put a damper on the date. She watched him inhale from his cheroot again, and wondered how he managed to get the smoke to go up his nose, and whether it was worse, cancer-wise, to inhale each hit twice?

The tourist family had fallen silent, and Ellen could feel them glaring at Potocka. The cheroot did stink—if it was a cheroot—but Ellen couldn't think of a polite way to tell Potocka to extinguish it.

Potocka crushed it out in a moment, anyway, and consulted the menu. Ellen picked hers up, too.

"What would you like?" said Potocka. "They have a lot of different things, although it is a little difficult for me to tell what each consists of . . . look here, we have something called a Maitri Casserole . . . do you know what this is?"

"It means 'friendliness,' " said Ellen. "In Sanskrit."

"Ah," said Potocka. "Aren't you a useful companion? A friendliness casserole. Very nice. And here, we have here a Yoni Salad. Do you know this word?"

If Potocka knew this word, he wasn't letting on. Ellen did not know much in the way of Sanskrit, but she did know what a *yoni* was, and she choked on the sip of water that she had just taken from her water glass.

"A Yoni Salad?"

"Yes," said Potocka, still looking at the menu. "Does that . . . er . . . ring a bell?"

"Sort of," said Ellen. "It probably has anchovies on it." And she felt the giggles well up in her throat. Don't laugh, she said to herself. Or you'll have to explain.

"Oh, I like anchovies," said Potocka innocently. "We shall try it," he decided. "A Yoni Salad, for an adventurous lunch, eh?"

"Okay," Ellen said.

Potocka ordered Yoni Salad for them both and turned his attention back to Ellen.

"So," he said.

"Ahem," said Ellen.

"It is uncomfortable, no?" said Potocka, laughing a little bit. "I don't know why. I am sorry."

"Oh, that's all right," said Ellen. "It's not your fault."

"We should converse," said Potocka.

"Converse?" said Ellen. *Converse!*

"Get to know each other."

"Yes," said Ellen. There was another awkward silence.

"Do you have any questions?" he asked.

Do I have any questions, Professor Potocka? Yes I do. Like: Why are you here? Why am *I* here? Why am I about to eat a salad, one named after what my mother would call "ladies' privates," with you?

"Um, no. I have no questions," said Ellen. "Unless . . . could you explain Ohm's Law to me?"

"Ohm's Law?" said Potocka, taken aback.

"Yes. I've always been a little confused about it . . ." said Ellen. "You know, about the electromotive force, and the electromagnetic resistance and all that . . . "

"If you want me to," said Potocka, "I will. But it isn't very interesting, I don't think. To tell you the truth, Ellen, I am very tired of electromagnetics."

"You are?" said Ellen.

"Ugh, yes," said Potocka. "I am tired of books and pencils, tired of learned conversation." (Oh, swell, thought Ellen.) "Couldn't we discuss something else, something more . . . personal?"

"Personal?" said Ellen. (*I'm writing a paper on the Song of Songs. Would you like to read it?*)

"Personal," Potocka repeated, hitching his chair a tiny bit closer to hers.

Clue in, girl, said Leona, from the back of Ellen's mind. Even I can figure this out: The guy may be an egghead, but he still wants to talk some wham-bam at you over your Yoni Salad.

Yes, I know. Maybe I should escape now? Feign nausea? I could walk up to the bookstore, instead. There is a good one, just two blocks from here. I haven't been to a good bookstore since Onion learned to grab and tear. Or I could hop a bus down to Georgetown, and pick up the course catalogue for the fall semester. (Onion, oh Onion. What is your Mommy doing?)

Potocka shifted casually in his chair. The fabric of Ellen's skirt rustled. His knee came close to hers without actually touching, and, by some means, pulled her knee irresistibly toward itself, and then made contact: Click!

Ahh, okay. Right.

A discussion of Genesis might have been a possibility at this point, Ellen supposed, but Potocka had relieved her of responsibility for a conversational topic: Leaning close, he'd begun to tell Ellen about, of all things, his mother.

"The woman was a saint," he said reverently, all the while transmitting his other, secular message through the closed circuit of their patellae. "A saint."

Of course, said Leona sourly. (Shut up, Leona. The man gives great knee.)

A saint, who died in the birthing of Potocka, back when the Nazis occupied Czechoslovakia, before the betrayal by the allies at Yalta, before the communists, Democracy with a Human Face, the death of Jan Masaryk and before the tanks that followed the Prague Spring.

(It was very interesting, Leona, I gotta admit. I was inspired, in fact, to inquire into recent Czech history. I had no idea it was so tumultuous, and tragic. Incidentally, did you know that Prague is pronounced Pra-hee, in Czech? You can't say that this date hasn't been educational so far.)

"I left after that," said Potocka. "She, my muzzer, is still buried there, near Prague. I should like to visit her grave. Do you have a wish to see Czechoslovakia, Ellen?"

"Um, Czechoslovakia?" said Ellen.

"Anything is possible," said Potocka.

Their waiter arrived with a tray, and Potocka moved away from Ellen, as though afraid the waiter might disapprove of their proximity. His knee went with him, and did not touch hers again, although Ellen's own knee fished for it under the table, almost of its own volition, for the remainder of the meal. The Yoni Salads turned out to be regular (slightly wilted) chef salads after all. Lots of slimy garbanzo beans, no anchovies. How disappointing, thought Ellen, wanting, again, to laugh.

"Muzzers, Ellen," Potocka was saying as their coffee arrived. "Food, muzzers, babies. These are the big things of life. Not

Ohm's Law. Not physics." He smiled at Ellen, and Ellen smiled back.

Ellen's possibilities loomed suddenly large before her, breathtaking, like this man's smile, and the energy that was radiating from him in her direction, pulling her in.

(Could I replace conversation, in my fantasies, with travel? she wondered. A nice trip to Pra-hee with Professor Potocka? I saw a movie once, where a couple screwed in the bathroom of an airplane. But I don't know if I would want to risk going at it in communist airspace. And, would I leave Onion with the stewardess?

What are you *talking* about, Ellen?)

After the salads, and coffee, Potocka paid the bill and they departed the Place of Peace. They walked along for a while without conversing. Ellen tried not to sweat. Potocka, who had not heretofore struck Ellen as particularly uncoordinated, bumped against her quite a lot. Shoulders and shoulders, hips and hips. Accidental, inevitable contacts: Oh yes, said Ellen to herself. *I remember this!*

He put his hand at the small of her back as they crossed Connecticut Avenue, and she let him.

"I am trying to woo you, Ellen," he said to her. "Is it working?"

Ellen thought about it. Her eyes slid sideways, up to catch his, and down again.

"Maybe," she said quietly.

He stopped in front of an apartment building, under a red awning.

"My home," he said, tilting his head toward the door. "You would like to come in? For a drink? I have beer."

"Uh . . . all right," said Ellen. "All right."

They walked through the lobby and down the hallway. It was a long dark hallway, with a red carpet and wallpaper that looked hairy. They stopped before a door at the far end, apartment number 10. A small white tag below the doorbell read: POTOCKA, A.

Potocka, *A?* Ellen thought. Oh yes, Albert. Bert is short for Albert.

"My flat," said Potocka.

"Right," said Ellen. "Listen, do you have a motorcycle?"

"A motorcycle?" said Potocka.

"Never mind," said Ellen. Scratch Ohm's Law, scratch the motorcycle. Scratch theology. It's time for beer and groping. I remember this, too.

"Come in," said Potocka. "Please."

Ellen did.

She found herself in a small room, a sort of foyer lined with bookshelves—homemade ones, from the looks of them, their pine boards sagging in the middle under the weight of heavy tomes. Ellen waited for Potocka to lead her elsewhere, but he did not. He closed the door, and stood in front of her. She looked upward into his expectant smile. I have seen that smile before, Ellen thought to herself. How familiar it is! *Go ahead,* it says. *Make my day.*

Ellen smiled back. Potocka reached and touched her face. With her chin in his palm, his fingers reached almost to her temples and his thumb was under her left ear.

What enormous hands you have, Potocka. Unless my head is shrinking. Like Alice in Wonderland nibbling the wrong mushroom.

"Such a face," Potocka said. "You look different without the baby, Ellen."

"Different?"

Potocka stood there, holding her face in one hand. Dear kindly God.

"You look younger, I meant. A young woman with a classic face. We should have to ask Botticelli to paint you today, not Raphael after all."

"Um, thank you," said Ellen. She tried to picture her own nose on a Botticelli nymph. "How nice of you to say so."

"I was married, too, once," he said suddenly.

"Oh?" said Ellen.

"I had a wife," he said, as though this was very unusual.

"I understand. And is she dead, also?" Ellen was prepared to be sympathetic.

Potocka laughed. "No, no. She left. She was a smart woman."

"Ah," said Ellen.

"Not smart to leave, I mean, although perhaps she was."

"Did you, um, have children?"

"No," said Potocka. "She didn't want to have them. Not with me, in any case. She left me for someone else, you know, someone not so much the workaholic."

"Ah," said Ellen. "I'm sorry."

"Yes, well. We all must find our own equilibrium. She needed to find hers, and knew it wasn't here, with Bert Potocka. As I say, a smart woman."

"God delights in oxymorons," said Ellen.

"Eh?" said Potocka, but he was distracted by then, stroking her cheek with concentration, as though its texture taught him something. "May I kiss you?"

Please.

"What?" said Ellen.

"Suddenly, I would like to kiss you," said Potocka. "I would like to, very much."

"Um, I see, " Ellen mumbled. Tasting his voice in her mouth. A voice like chocolate, and Ellen felt the old, slow spiral of desire begin inside of her, winding its way up under her ribs toward her throat. There was a tingling in her breasts—oh, Christ, was her milk letting down?

"Sometimes it is like that," Potocka was saying. "Like a lodestone and iron, you know? Not often, but sometimes."

"Sometimes what is like what?" said Ellen, confused, because Potocka had moved closer. He smelled, not like chocolate, but rather like Ellen's elementary school; clean, but with a whiff of pencil shavings and something else: graham crackers or Old Spice. Or tobacco?

"What is a lodestone?" said Ellen.

"A piece of magnetic iron ore which is found magnetized in its natural state. Hah! Ellen! You will not make me lecture you now, will you?"

"Not if you don't want to," said Ellen.

"I don't want to," said Potocka. "Not at all."

Damn it to hell. She was leaking like a cow at milking time. Maybe I could run to his bathroom real quick, and express myself? she thought. Oh Lordy, but she couldn't run anywhere. Couldn't run, could barely stand. She was a lodestone, he said. Was that a compliment? He seemed to intend it as such.

"You smell like school," she said faintly. "It's nice."

"I am a teacher," he replied, with both hands on her face, now, tilting it gently as though searching for its perfect angle, and his mouth was close to hers. Ellen's back was against the door, and her face was swallowed in his hands.

Yes, kiss me. If you don't kiss me right now, Potocka, you bastard, I'm going to die. Or drown in milk.

"Um," said Ellen again. Tilting her chin. Opening her mouth.

"Perhaps not," Bert decided briskly, dropping his hands to his sides and leaving Ellen's face cold.

"What?" Ellen squeaked, and Potocka laughed.

"Oh, Ellen. Perhaps no kisses, eh? This is too fast. We must know each other better yet. Come in here, and sit down. Not to worry. You would like a beer?"

Was this some twisted Czech perversion, to torture a married woman, to make a mother leak at the breast, to tease?

"A beer?"

"Yes, a But-Viser? Is that okay?"

"Oh yes, fine. Beer is fine," said Ellen, trying not to actually pant. "I like beer. Besides, a little brewskie might make the baby sleep better tonight, too."

"I beg your pardon?" said Potocka, clearly uninformed about the transmission of alcohol into the breast milk of nursing mothers.

"Never mind," said Ellen.

Potocka ushered her into another, larger room, obviously the living room in what seemed to be an even smaller dwelling than the one Ellen shared with her family.

"Don't go away," said Potocka and went to fetch some But-Viser.

Ellen looked around. The room she was in looked like Potocka's Georgetown office. Most of the space was taken up by a large desk strewn with papers and books and assortments of writing utensils bitten and chewed into near-uselessness. There were photographs of various people thumbtacked on one wall; gatherings of bearded men, one fat, scowling teenager (a nephew? Potocka himself?), miscellaneous women, a picture of Potocka in front of Karl Marx's tomb. There were a few leaflets announcing lectures in physics, there were postcards, including one of a painting of the Madonna and Child. Ellen tipped it up on its Scotch-taped hinge, read the caption: BY RAPHAEL. Of course. There was no writing on the back. Ellen felt suddenly, acutely uncomfortable, as though she had come across a photograph of herself in this virtual stranger's possession.

She let the postcard flip back down. She sat down on the couch.

"Here we have a series of images, from the early and late Renaissance, of the Madonna and Child," one of her theology professors spoke from Ellen's memory. "Look at them. What do you see? Madonna, child. Grapes. Wheat. These, in the company of humbled kings, these enshrined, encrusted with gold, rendered in the finest techniques and materials available to the artist and his patron: these ordinary things, mother, child, wine, bread."

Ellen heard a refrigerator door opening and closing, and the *pop . . . ahhh, pop . . . ahhh* as Potocka uncapped the bottles of beer. She could feel the tension in him even from another room, as though her body were a compass needle turning itself slowly southward, toward a new signal.

Potocka returned with two open bottles.

"Here," he said, handing one to Ellen and taking a deep suck of the other. "Drink up."

Ellen took a cautious sip.

"You don't like But-Viser?" said Potocka anxiously.

"It's fine," said Ellen. "I love it."

"What do you think of my place?"

"It's . . . well, it's very nice," said Ellen.

"Yes, well, it needs the feminine touch," said Potocka, shaking his head. "I don't have much time or inclination for decorations."

"I see," said Ellen, trying her best to look as though she, herself, had the time or inclination for decorations.

"A woman could do a lot with this place," Potocka was saying. He gazed fondly at Ellen. Oh, Lord, Ellen thought. Is that what he had in mind? Was all that business about kissing just a trick, to get me to help him choose some wallpaper or something? And what about taking me to Czechoslovakia? (Will we ever get around to discussing physics? she wondered. Or will he tell me about the rest of his relatives, instead?)

"You need to water your spider plant," she said helpfully.

"Yes. But not now," said Potocka. He took Ellen's bottle from her, and put it down beside his on the coffee table. He sat down beside her. Ellen tried not to look at him, tried not to taste his voice in her mouth. She tried not to think about kissing, or chocolate, or screwing on airplanes.

"Where, um, did the child abuser live?" she asked, then.

"Who?" said Potocka.

"You know, the guy who beat his kids? The one you had to testify against?" said Ellen.

"Oh. Oh, yes. Next door," said Potocka, gesturing behind them. "Through that wall. I could hear him, day after day. Shouting and striking, throwing things. Like a man possessed. He was quite a wealthy man, too, apparently. He worked for the government, I was told. And his children, crying, a sound to torment you . . . . I can never understand things like that . . . I thought I would be sick. I am not good with violence, Ellen, even in the movies. I was so glad when the police arrived."

I know the feeling, Ellen thought.

"It was good of you to get involved," said Ellen. "Saul . . . my husband, he . . . um . . . says many people ignore these things."

"I don't understand that, either. But let's not talk about it now, Ellen. It is so sad to think of it. That poor family has moved away, perhaps to something better. We can hope."

"Yes," said Ellen.

Potocka put his arm around her. Ellen studied her hands. They looked unnaturally small and pale where they lay, nested like two white mice in her lap. She had a sudden image of Leona's hands, of the V-shaped scar on Leona's brown knuckle. Potocka pulled Ellen toward him, tucking her in beneath his arm. His face was close enough to her for his breath to disturb the fine hair at the back of her neck.

"You are so quiet, Ellen," said Potocka. Inhaling and exhaling sex into her ear. Ellen closed her eyes. "So quiet. You are wonderful. I want to kiss you."

I am not wonderful, Ellen thought.

"I won't stop, this time," said Potocka. "I promise."

"I know you won't," Ellen whispered. Her eyes still closed.

"What are you thinking about?" said Potocka.

Your mouth. Your mouth, and chocolate voice.

Chapter XIV

"What are you thinking about?" said the Potocka of her imagination. "This God of yours, again? This union of opposites, this yin-yang deity . . ."

"But it isn't a union of opposites," Ellen interrupted him. "Not of *opposites*. That would require that I think of women as being the opposite of men, black the opposite of white, self the opposite of other, and I don't. Opposites can interlock, but they can never merge, the other never becomes part of the self, even imaginatively. When a culture grounds its philosophy in a system of opposites, it is inevitable that whoever is in charge of parceling out the supposedly mutually exclusive qualities will save the nicer or more interesting ones for those like himself. Or herself."

"Then what are men and women, if not opposites?" said Potocka. "What is the sexual union in Genesis, if not the union of opposites?"

"Men and women are the same," said Ellen, "in every way except that their selves reside in different bodies, which makes certain aspects of life, and perhaps all of life, a necessarily different experience for a woman than it is for a man. Not an

opposite experience, just a different one. The flow of blood,
for instance, is always a sign of injury to a man. For women, it
is sometimes a sign of injury, sometimes a sign of reproductive
health. Pain, likewise, is usually a sign of injury, but for women
it is also a normal accompaniment to a healthy birth.

"And while women live in bodies that can or must be shared
with another, separate being, men always have their bodies to
themselves.

"And so on.

"Nonetheless, we must attempt to share and reconcile the
experiences of men and women, and not only sexually. If
sexual union, a union of bodies, was all that was required, then
any heterosexual coupling would image God, and this clearly
isn't the case. Something else has to happen, in sex . . . "

"O sex!" Potocka said longingly, but Ellen, as usual, wasn't
listening to him.

" . . . or in art, or any other endeavor toward God's image,
something that makes the effort more than just itself. It isn't
as easy as putting opposites side by side (perhaps with some
token reference to the Other within the Self: the discreet and
separate portion of light within the dark portion of the yin-yang
symbol, for instance, and the dark within the light). It is as
difficult as pushing your imagination out until you recognize
the inclusion of otherness within yourself, that their vulnerability or violence belongs to you, that their maleness or
femaleness is in you with definitions blurred, it is as difficult
as excluding *no one* from your God however you envision Her.
Your sex, your race and all the other accidental circumstances
of your life might affect how you approach God, what work you
do in Her name, and with whom, but none of these will alter
how God approaches you. God is incapable of exclusion on any
grounds because God is, by definition, inclusive: God is the
anthropomorphized event of total inclusion and that is how and
why we must worship Her. *There is neither Jew nor Greek, there*

is neither slave nor free, there is neither male nor female; for you are all one in Christ Jesus.

"But in fact, even if we take only heterosexuality as our example, we can see that since Genesis, with few exceptions (the Song of Songs being a notable and surprising one) the exclusions, distortions and perversions that the patriarchal tradition's hatred and disdain for women (whether encoded or explicit) forced upon the sexual relationship actually prevented the sexual relationship from being what it could be: a model for human relationships, including the relationship with the self. Genuine heterosexual intimacy is probably the most difficult imaginable relationship: Even in the absence of stereotypes and prejudice there is no human difference as primary and inescapable as that of gender. Yet it is of each other that men and women are meant to say: *This is flesh of my flesh, bone of my bone.* If a man and a woman can be genuinely united, united before God, or, to put it another way, if the Ha'adam can be re-united, whole and round, then *anyone* can.

"God made it hard for us, when She split the Earth Creature. When all the differences between us, not just sex, but race and, for that matter, the infinite variations and permutations of personality, of visions, capacities and desires that make it hard to find union even with those like oneself were brought into being, God made creating Her image in the conduct of an ordinary everyday human life a matter of effort. It is meant to be hard, to involve sacrifice. Why on earth would receiving God's blessings be as easy as only saying the right words once a week, when our well-lived lives would be the finer prayer? And why, while we're on the subject, should God be something that blesses us outright, when it makes so much more sense that She would have encoded our blessings in the richness of our human intercourses, that we are meant to be *each other's* blessings? Our redemption lies in reunion, and a profound intimacy between a man and a woman can be a redeeming experience, a reunion not only with each other but, through this, with God. It is difficult because it is meant to be, this intimacy I mean . . . or I suppose I might mean . . . well, you know. *Marriage?*

"I do mean marriage, don't I? Marriage, of course. The way marriage could be, if one were to follow through on all the promises made at the beginning. Yes, I think this might be: That your ordinary, run-of-the-mill marriage might be vital after all. Difficult, of course, but what makes it difficult must also be what makes marriage sacred."

"Mothers, children, wine, bread. We must find the sacred in our ordinary lives," said Ellen's theology professor. "We must live it in our ordinary lives."

Okay, said Ellen. Like in a marriage, for instance. Marriage in the particular: Saul and me.

Saul and me.

"Ahah," said Ellen. "A ton is a ton is a ton."

· — · — · — · —

"I beg your pardon?" he said, softly into the back of her neck, and Ellen blinked. There he was. Not at all resembling the Potocka in her mind, who didn't look like anyone, anymore. This Potocka was real, with a real body emitting real heat.

Something was wrong. Something about the name Albert, or the postcard on the wall, or the spider plant dying on the window ledge.

"God!" said Potocka. "Is it always so difficult to drag the words from you? You are not exactly . . . what do they call it? A chatterbox."

"Um," said Ellen.

Why is it that everyone but me knows what to want? she asked herself. And why am I suddenly aware of myself, of *my* own real body; of my heat and cycle, the glands in my breasts producing milk, of my womb with its cargo of blood and memories, good and bad?

Ellen remembered the intensity of new kisses, and that intensity alone might have been worth turning her head to rediscover, even had Potocka not been as attractive as he was. She remembered the novel power of Leona's mouth, for instance, and of the other men's mouths before that, she remembered her body pressed between Frederick O. Plimpton's body and the wall of the medical school classroom, remembered him taking her face in his hands as Potocka had done in the foyer, or as Saul had done, her darling Saul, O Saul! in love and in labor . . .

. . . there isn't a lot of variation in what bodies do, is there, Mom? Ellen thought.

Not a whole lot, my daughter. It might be easier if there were.

We are married. Saul and I.

But it is uncomfortable, and difficult.

Do you believe what you are saying, Ellen Elliot, or don't you?

Oh, hell, said Ellen. I do.

"Perhaps you are one of the world's listeners," said Potocka. Ellen did not turn her head, but she laughed out loud.

"You laugh," said Potocka, in his beautiful voice. "Are you thinking of love? I am thinking of love."

"I am thinking of love," said Ellen. "Sort of."

He had apparently given up on waiting for the opportunity to kiss her. Instead, he leaned down and rested his head on Ellen's chest, with the top of it just under her chin. Ellen did not know how to remove his head from her chest without seeming rude. She looked down, and saw where the hair grew out of his scalp.

"Oh, Ellen, Ellen," Bert was saying into her shirt. "When I first saw you, with your child in your arms, I knew you were for me. Such a warm, quiet, muzzerly girl. I have wanted a muzzerly girl so much."

Muzzerly? Ellen thought. What does he mean, muzzerly?

Motherly! He means *motherly*!

Ellen started to laugh again, but she caught it, and did her best to swallow it down into her throat. Motherly! she thought, her chest heaving.

Bert, under the impression that the commotion under his ear was due to different causes, said: "You want love. Oh, Ellen. I knew you would."

Hilarity mistaken for desire, said Leona, from somewhere in Sisterspace. That's heterosexuality for you.

I can't let him know my body, Leona. And he would if we . . .

Screwed, said Leona. But wasn't that the idea? You bought all of that snazzy underwear, after all.

Or even if we talked, Leona. He would have to know my scars, only he wasn't there when Onion was born. He wasn't there when they took Onion from my opened belly, and he doesn't know, the way Saul knows, why mine is a beautiful scar after all.

Oh, God, Leona, I am married after all. I have really married Saul, not once but a thousand times, and lo-and-behold I am going to have to do it again today.

"Potocka," she said.

"Bert," said Potocka. "Call me Bert." He spoke softly into her left breast.

I miss Saul, Ellen thought. I miss him. I want my own man, who has seen my blood, who has seen our baby born, who knows things I don't know: the shape of my womb, and the look of Onion when his face was first brought to light. I want to talk to Saul.

"Something is not right, here," she said aloud.

"What do you mean?" said Potocka, and his voice sounded suddenly wary, although his head was still on her breast.

"I'm married," said Ellen.

"I know that," said Potocka. "Don't worry about it." He was fiddling with the buttons of her shirt.

What do I do with my body and my mind, Mom?

Work at it. Not this way. Find another way, and work hard.
It is what women do, said Ellen's mother. Or, they try to.

And men, too?

When they see the schism. It isn't as clear for them, is it?
Men, with their impenetrable bodies, their unimpregnable,
unoccupiable bodies, bodies not inescapably constructed for
the accommodation of another. But the schism is real, and the
recognition of it is a blessing, of sorts, my daughter. A blessing
for women, and you might as well see it that way, as there are
precious few blessings coming our way. We take what we can
get, said Maude.

Although it is hard, said Leona.

No matter what, said Maude.

No deseamos nada más, said Grummy.

Ellen realized, at this point, both that Potocka was about to
pop the fastening of her very damp brassiere, and that she was
patting his back with the same, absentminded, businesslike
briskness that she normally used on Onion after a feed. The
patting had the same effect on the professor as it usually did
on Onion: that is, Potocka burped.

Ellen stood up, abruptly, and Bert Potocka almost fell off
the couch.

"*What?*" he said, trying to get his legs under control.
"What?"

"I'm terribly sorry," said Ellen. "But I've changed my mind."

"Because of my belch?"

"No, no," said Ellen impatiently. "Of course not."

"But you wanted love! I know you did, I could see it in your
eyes, and hear it in the wild beating of your heart."

"Well, yes," said Ellen. "I did want love. Or whatever I
wanted, I did want it. I have to admit that. But I am married.
More married than I thought."

"I don't understand," said Bert.

"It doesn't matter," said Ellen. "I can't explain it anyway. It's
religious."

"What is religious?"

"Marriage," said Ellen. "It's sacred, even."

"Oh, Christ," said Potocka.

"I'm sorry," said Ellen again. Backing up, moving for the hallway. "But listen, Potocka, Bert I mean, listen, the main thing is, I'm really not the right woman for you. I might have been, once, but I'm not any longer. I'm not what I used to be."

"But you were, before. Out there in the foyer. You can't tell me you weren't interested then, can you? I should have made my feverish love to you there, eh? While I had the chance? Oh, God, it is always a mistake to *converse*!"

"No no," said Ellen, not allowing herself to be distracted by the image of Potocka's making feverish love to her between badly made pine bookcases. "No, Bert, it is never a mistake to converse. Besides, this has nothing to do with that. And you are . . . you know. Nice. I like you. I like you very much. You're . . . well, you are very sexy. Astonishingly sexy, in fact . . . "

Potocka got up off the floor.

" . . . et cetera. But I can't do anything with you. It all has to do with Genesis," said Ellen quickly, to quell any lingering hopes he may have had.

"Genesis?" said Potocka.

"Never mind. You don't want to know."

"I might."

"Yes," said Ellen, regarding him thoughtfully. "You might. But I can't stay here and tell you. Okay? I'm sorry."

"If you say so," said Potocka dubiously, but not without dignity. He walked her courteously to the door of his apartment. They stood for a moment in the hallway. Potocka looked at Ellen. Ellen smiled politely at Potocka's books.

"Michael Faraday," she said, pointing to a title. "Who is that?"

"Look it up," said Potocka, the way teachers do.

"Okay," said Ellen. She shook his hand awkwardly and said: "Good-bye."

"Good-bye," said Potocka, holding fast to her fingers with flattering regret. "If you ever change your mind, Ellen, you know where I am."

"Good-bye," said Ellen again.

She walked very quickly from Potocka's door down the red and hairy hallway. He watched her go, but Ellen did not turn around. She was unaware of his eyes, in fact, and was thinking about something else entirely by the time she reached the white heat of Connecticut Avenue. She trotted past the zoo and the library, and up Macomb Street. She didn't stop until she got to the playground.

The child and her mother were gone. Ellen could see small footprints and the tracks of the toy truck in the sand.

Hi, Dad, she said to the sandbox. I should have brought some flowers for you.

Ellen washed her face in the drinking fountain. She sat down on a swing. She kicked herself slowly back and forth. Dust rose in whirls around her feet and settled on her pale shaved legs, disguising their nudity.

I have to go back to school, she thought. Like Leona.

We have to stop questioning our bodies, Leona, both of us. What is profane, she said to herself—sex, that is—our bodies, our blood and lives, is sacred, and the commitments we make with our bodies are sacred. Difficult, and sacred.

Saul, she thought. I love Saul.

This at last is flesh of my flesh and bone of my bone.

I thought I had time for it, for Potocka, for all of that, but I don't. It isn't my time for suggestive voices inhaling and exhaling sex, for screwing strangers, on soccer fields, on airplanes or in foyers. I am finished with sex as a question. I have an answer, now.

It was a leap in the darkness to marry him. How extraordinary, that I should have leaped in the right direction? And slid back, perhaps, but leaped again, toward the piece of the Garden I have in Saul.

Ellen pushed herself backward with her heels in the dirt, leaning back, looking up.

If you are showered with blessings, your first duty before God is to recognize and accept as many of them as you can, and not struggle against what is yours from Her. I am surrounded by flowers: Saul and my butter-colored son. I am blessed beyond words.

The swing caught Ellen in her fall and lifted her toward the pale leaves that shivered on the same trees that had been there when she was a child.

And your second duty before God, Ellen said severely to herself, as the swing dropped her back towards the ground, is to be a blessing to someone else. I am already a blessing to Onion, by instinct, but I must apply myself to being a blessing to Saul. *At least* to Saul. At least as much as he is a blessing to me.

Maybe I'll go to divinity school and become a minister. Hee hee! Then I can talk and talk all Sunday morning, and a whole churchful of folk will listen devotedly.

("Hell, why not," said Leona, later, when Ellen called her with this possibility. "I'd go for it.")

There was a cramp, just then, in her belly. Menstruation after all, she thought, feeling the first wet seep between her legs (thinking fleetingly, and without regret, of her peach satin undies iced with an inch of white lace). Well, well. That means I have been ovulating, it means there is room in me. Even for another baby. Wrap your mind around that one, Saul, with your hip that smells of sweet gun oil and your good, stout, father's heart. How fatherly do you want to be?

As fatherly as I am muzzerly? Ellen laughed at that, laughed to herself and at herself all the way from the playground to her mother's house, where her first child waited, an incarnation in his own round self of everything good that had ever befallen Ellen Elliot.

·—·—·—·—·

"Ma ma!" said Onion, smiling all over with his own electric rapture when Ellen arrived. "Ma ma!"

"Saul called," said Maude. "He says he'll be home at four, for certain."

"Good," said Ellen. "Oh, that's good."

"Why are you beaming like that?" said Maude. "One would think you had been apart from him for months."

"Seems like it," said Ellen.

"Huh," said Maude. "Young love. There's nothing more revolting. He says you are thinking of going back to school, is that right? It's a good idea, Ellen, and long overdue. There's nothing wrong with your mind, you know. And you will need a way to be useful, after Onion has gone on in the world. I think I might as well go back to school, too. If you want to know the truth, I've resigned myself to Spanish lessons." She looked ruefully at Grummy, who was kissing Onion good-bye. "Onion said *sí* today, when I asked him if he wanted a cookie."

"If you can't beat 'em, join 'em." Ellen picked Onion up, and inhaled his fresh pumpkin smell when he pushed his face against her throat. "*Ma ma ma ma,*" said Onion.

"Are you going to weep?" said Maude.

"Just this once, I think," said Ellen.

She carried her son down the front steps to the car. She buckled him carefully into his car seat. She touched his soft hair, hair the color of butter.

"Do you want to see Da da?" she asked him.

"*Sí!* Da da!" said Onion, raising one finger in preparation for pointing at his father. "Da da?"

"He'll be home before we are," Ellen assured him, and Saul was.

"*Yo creía que habría más tiempo,*" said Grummy, as they watched Ellen drive away.

"Yes," said Maude. "*Sí.*"